Alexander Thom und Co.

Irisch Land Commission

Judicial Rents

Alexander Thom und Co.

Irisch Land Commission
Judicial Rents

ISBN/EAN: 9783742802484

Manufactured in Europe, USA, Canada, Australia, Japa

Cover: Foto ©Andreas Hilbeck / pixelio.de

Manufactured and distributed by brebook publishing software
(www.brebook.com)

Alexander Thom und Co.

Irisch Land Commission

Irish Land Commission.

Land Law Acts.

RETURN

ACCORDING TO PROVINCES AND COUNTIES

OF

JUDICIAL RENTS

FIXED BY

SUB-COMMISSIONS AND CIVIL BILL COURTS,

FOR FIRST AND SECOND STATUTORY TERMS,

AS NOTIFIED TO THE IRISH LAND COMMISSION DURING THE MONTH OF

MARCH, 1897.

Presented to both Houses of Parliament by Command of Her Majesty.

DUBLIN:
PRINTED FOR HER MAJESTY'S STATIONERY OFFICE,
BY ALEXANDER THOM & CO. (LIMITED).

And to be purchased, either directly or through any Bookseller, from
HODGES, FIGGIS and Co. (LIMITED), 104, Grafton-street, Dublin: or
EYRE and SPOTTISWOODE, East Harding-street, Fleet-street, E.C.; or
JOHN MENZIES and Co. 12, Hanover-street, Edinburgh, and 90, West Nile-street, Glasgow.

1897.

INDEX.

SUMMARIES FOR MARCH, 1897.

FIRST STATUTORY TERM.

Summary showing, according to Provinces and Counties, the Number of Cases in which Judicial Rents have been Fixed by Sub-Commissioners under the Land Law (Ireland) Act, 1881, for a *First Statutory Term*, during the Month of March, 1897; and also the Acreage, Tenement Valuations, Former Rents, and Judicial Rents of the Holdings.

Province and County.	Number of Cases in which Judicial Rents have been fixed.	Acreage.			Tenement Valuation.			Former Rent.			Judicial Rent.		
		a.	r.	p.	£	s.	d.	£	s.	d.	£	s.	d.
ULSTER—		Statute Measure.											
Antrim,	8	143	0	1	63	5	0	80	6	1	64	6	0
Armagh,	18	373	3	34	109	15	0	96	20	7	64	13	9
Cavan,	13	201	1	31	119	13	0	126	11	3	95	1	4
Donegal,	14	1,273	1	7	541	1	4	641	16	11	618	3	5
Down,	79	534	3	23	363	0	0	380	17	8	330	13	6
Fermanagh,	57	929	3	25	613	13	0	545	19	9	619	6	4
Londonderry,	1	143	3	37	105	7	0	104	11	8	75	1	4
Monaghan,	13	273	1	1	175	8	0	171	8	8	113	1	9
Tyrone,	16	407	1	25	846	0	0	960	13	9	199	13	0
Total,	208	3,893	8	10	2,469	7	8	3,356	19	6	1,733	3	3
LEINSTER—													
Dublin,	24	648	3	39	970	0	0	1,162	12	10	937	19	3
Longford,	1	73	1	10	48	5	0	53	14	9	43	14	0
Queen's,	9	743	1	21	134	10	0	138	10	3	126	10	9
Westmeath,	7	93	2	23	7	0	0	37	10	0	29	13	0
Total,	51	1,573	1	22	1,163	13	0	1,406	16	9	1,700	0	3
MUNSTER—													
Clare,	10	198	3	37	123	3	0	157	15	8	108	17	0
Cork,	8	450	1	17	870	0	0	304	1	10	248	18	6
Kerry,	1	91	7	14	24	15	0	34	0	0	33	0	9
Tipperary,	1	10	3	31	11	0	0	17	0	0	10	3	0
Total,	20	771	8	17	429	18	0	516	17	6	349	0	8

IRELAND.

ULSTER,	208	3,893	3	10	2,469	7	8	3,356	19	6	1,733	3	3
LEINSTER,	54	1,573	1	22	1,149	13	0	1,406	16	9	1,300	0	3
MUNSTER,	20	770	2	17	429	16	0	516	17	6	349	0	8
TOTALS,	280	6,045	2	9	5,048	0	8	4,280	8	8	5,807	3	3

NOTE.—There were no Judicial Rents fixed upon the Reports of Valuers during this month.

CIVIL BILL COURTS.

SUMMARY FOR MARCH, 1897.

FIRST STATUTORY TERM.

Cases in which Judicial Rents have been Fixed by Civil Bill Courts, under the Land Law (Ireland) Act, 1891, for a *First Statutory Term*, and notified to the Irish Land Commission during the Month of March, 1897.

Province and County.	Number of Cases in which Judicial Rents have been fixed.	Acreage.	Previous Valuation.	Former Rent.	Judicial Rent.
		Statute Measure.			
		A. R. P.	£ s. d.	£ s. d.	£ s. d.
ULSTER — Armagh,	3	6 3 0	13 10 0	8 10 0	8 7 6
LEINSTER —					
Kilkenny,	1	44 0 0	17 0 0	16 0 0	15 0 0
Louth,	14	244 0 34	184 4 0	344 5 0	194 13 0
Westmeath,	2	65 1 7	33 4 0	79 18 0	71 0 0
Total,	17	303 2 5	233 10 0	390 3 0	277 13 0
CONNAUGHT — Leitrim,	8	203 0 0	76 0 0	63 6 6	30 14 6
MUNSTER — Cork,	6	186 2 17	127 15 0	163 15 6	113 13 0

IRELAND.

ULSTER,	3	6 3 0	13 10 0	8 10 0	8 7 6
LEINSTER,	17	303 2 5	233 10 0	390 3 0	277 13 0
CONNAUGHT,	8	203 0 0	76 0 0	63 6 6	30 14 6
MUNSTER,	6	186 2 17	127 15 0	163 15 6	113 13 0
Totals,	34	704 2 31	451 15 0	651 1 10	300 8 0

LEASEHOLDERS.

FIRST STATUTORY TERM.

SUMMARY FOR MARCH, 1897.

Summary showing, according to Provinces and Counties, the Number of Cases in which Judicial Rents have been Fixed by Sub-Commissions, under the Land Law (Ireland) Act, 1887, and the Redemption of Rent (Ireland) Act, 1891, for a *First Statutory Term*, during the Month of March, 1897; and also the Acreages, Tenement Valuations, Former Rents, and Judicial Rents of the Holdings.

Province and County.	Number of Cases in which Judicial Rents have been fixed	Acreage.			Tenement Valuation.			Former Rent.			Judicial Rent.		
		A.	R.	P.	£	s.	d.	£	s.	d.	£	s.	d.
ULSTER —													
Armagh,	1	19	3	31	—			19	11	10	17	15	11
Cavan,	1	11	3	16	10	10	0	9	10	1	8	0	4
Donegal,	3	103	2	33	45	6	0	80	9	0	64	14	5
Down,	3	92	0	6	110	5	0	105	9	11	62	3	0
Fermanagh,	1	21	1	30	15	15	0	14	10	0	11	4	4
Londonderry,	1	40	1	10	71	0	0	36	7	0	34	14	0
Total,	9	289	1	9	246	15	0	340	17	10	113	3	1
LEINSTER —													
Dublin,	4	246	1	26	231	0	0	322	0	0	247	18	0
Queen's,	1	143	1	27	—			116	6	11	64	4	4
Wicklow,	1	106	3	39	223	10	0	371	8	4	300	0	4
Total,	6	546	3	10	454	10	0	831	15	3	634	4	1
MUNSTER —													
Clare,	3	427	0	26	123	10	0	180	8	0	105	5	6
Cork,	6	197	2	9	146	0	0	149	17	4	137	9	0
Total,	7	624	3	35	269	10	0	350	2	6	243	1	6

IRELAND.

Province.		Number	Acreage			Tenement Valuation			Former Rent			Judicial Rent		
ULSTER,	—	9	289	1	9	246	15	0	340	17	10	173	9	1
LEINSTER,	—	6	546	3	10	456	10	0	831	15	6	634	4	0
MUNSTER,	—	7	624	3	35	269	10	0	350	2	4	243	1	0
TOTALS,	—	21	1,470	3	14	974	15	0	1,542	15	5	1,049	14	1

CIVIL BILL COURTS.

LEASEHOLDERS.

FIRST STATUTORY TERM.

SUMMARY FOR MARCH, 1897.

Cases in which Judicial Rents have been Fixed by Civil Bill Courts under the Land Law (Ireland) Act, 1887, for a *First Statutory Term*, and notified to the Irish Land Commission, during the Month of March, 1897.

Province and County.	Number of Cases in which Judicial Rents have been Fixed.	Acreage.	Tenement Valuation.	Former Rent.	Judicial Rent.
		Statute Measure.			
		A. R. P.	£ s. d.	£ s. d.	£ s. d.
ULSTER.—					
Cork, ...	3	233 0 20	34 5 0	37 0 0	63 17 6

IRELAND.

SUMMARIES FOR MARCH, 1897.

SECOND STATUTORY TERM.

Summary showing, according to Provinces and Counties, the Number of Cases in which Judicial Rents have been Fixed by Sub-Commissioners under the Land Law (Ireland) Act, 1881, for a Second Statutory Term, during the Month of March, 1897; and also the Average Tenement Valuations, Rents of the Holdings prior to the creation of First Statutory Term, Judicial Rents for First Statutory Term, and the Judicial Rents for a Second Statutory Term.

Provinces and County.	Number of Cases in which Judicial Rents were fixed.	Acreage.			Tenement Valuation.			Rent of Holdings Prior to creation of First Statutory Term.			Judicial Rent for First Statutory Term.			Judicial Rent for Second Statutory Term.		
		Imeum Acreage.			£	s.	d.	£	s.	d.	£	s.	d.	£	s.	d.
		A.	R.	P.												
ULSTER—																
Antrim,	63	1,597	1	14	1,163	19	9	1,590	16	10	1,194	14	0	778	5	1
Armagh,	74	3,337	1	5	1,069	13	8	1,301	4	8	923	1	0	650	4	1
Cavan,	66	7,351	2	7	765	10	0	1,063	10	11	835	4	5	611	15	6
Donegal,	81	3,075	3	10	1,304	17	0	1,613	13	7	1,725	5	0	863	1	5
Down,	150	1,667	7	16	3,940	5	0	3,334	19	11	3,638	6	4	1,967	11	10
Fermanagh,	17	2,113	3	43	1,301	1	0	1,578	7	5	1,177	6	8	916	4	1
Londonderry,	23	1,133	3	50	669	15	0	836	10	7	206	0	0	611	4	1
Monaghan,	87	1,451	3	53	1,015	0	0	1,798	16	0	1,015	17	5	738	12	1
Tyrone,	113	5,265	7	91	1,811	16	1	2,196	0	1	1,584	13	0	1,165	5	1
Total,	745	17,975	3	33	11,739	15	10	14,958	17	3	11,635	13	1	8,361	10	1
LEINSTER—																
Dublin,	9	157	0	5	188	15	0	796	4	11	791	10	0	723	4	8
Longford,	25	901	7	78	551	15	0	951	4	2	895	0	0	539	17	4
Queen's,	30	1,413	0	20	827	10	0	1,516	11	11	1,184	0	0	717	10	4
Total,	64	2,331	3	38	1,543	0	0	3,597	1	0	3,191	10	0	1,979	11	4
MUNSTER—																
Clare,	33	1,731	1	8	543	17	0	960	8	3	746	0	0	599	5	1
Cork,	7	404	3	21	303	5	0	448	4	5	393	0	0	301	4	1
Kerry,	5	304	3	21	143	6	0	349	0	0	379	0	0	144	11	9
Tipperary,	1	116	0	0	96	0	0	184	9	4	160	0	0	103	9	1
Total,	46	2,316	3	11	1,119	8	0	1,941	5	2	1,529	0	0	1,117	15	1

IRELAND.

ULSTER,	745	17,915	3	33	11,739	15	10	14,958	17	3	11,635	15	1	6,361	10	1
LEINSTER,	64	2,333	3	30	1,543	0	0	3,597	1	0	3,194	10	0	1,979	17	4
MUNSTER,	46	2,346	3	11	1,149	6	0	1,591	5	2	1,529	0	0	1,117	15	1
Total,	855	22,695	1	34	14,431	1	10	19,516	8	4	16,372	5	1	11,159	8	1

CIVIL BILL COURTS.

SUMMARY FOR MARCH, 1897.

Cases in which Judicial Rents have been fixed by Civil Bill Courts, under the Land Law (Ireland) Act, 1881, for a *Second Statutory Term*, and notified to the Irish Land Commission during the Month of March, 1897.

Province and County.	Number of Cases in which Judicial Rents have been fixed.	Acreage.			Tenement Valuation			Rent of Holdings Prior to Creation of the First Statutory Term.			Judicial Rent for First Statutory Term.			Judicial Rent for a Second Statutory Term.		
		Statute Measure.			£ s. d.			£ s. d.			£ s. d.			£ s. d.		
		A. R. P.														
Leinster — Clare, ...	9	294 3 15			128 5 0			177 4 6			153 6 8			105 10 0		
Leinster — Louth, ...	2	21 1 16			20 15 0			29 6 6			23 10 0			16 6 0		
Connaught — Leitrim, ...	17	465 0 12			125 5 0			195 15 2			156 9 6			89 5 0		
Munster — Cork, ...	20	1,127 1 10			645 10 0			998 7 6			878 17 8			837 8 0		
Waterford, ...	1	141 7 5			96 15 0			144 10 6			117 0 0			47 8 0		
Total, ...	31	1,783 3 15			760 5 0			1,143 18 0			955 17 8			884 16 0		

IRELAND.

ULSTER, ...	9	294 6 23			128 5 0			177 4 4			153 4 6			105 10 0		
LEINSTER, ...	2	21 1 16			20 15 0			29 6 6			23 10 0			16 6 0		
CONNAUGHT, ...	17	455 0 12			125 5 0			195 18 2			156 9 6			89 5 0		
MUNSTER, ...	21	1,263 8 15			760 4 0			1,143 16 0			995 17 6			884 16 0		
TOTALS, ...	49	2,045 0 23			1,034 9 0			1,545 2 2			1,329 1 8			905 17 0		

FIRST STATUTORY TERM.

PROVINCE OF

COUNTY OF

Names of Assistant Commissioners by whom Cases were decided.	Record Number	Date of Order.	Name of Tenant.	Name of Landlord.	Townland.
Assistant Commissioners—		1887.			
D. TIGHE (Legal). THOS. DAVIDSON. G. H. SCULLEN.	8567	March 16.	Abraham M'Thomson,	F. A. D. Crummlin, —	Cherry End, ...
W. F. BAILEY (Legal), W. H. C. EYRE. J. ABERNETHY.	3356	March 28.	Philip Corkin,	LA-Gen, T. H. Pakenham, D.L.	Ballyshanagh,
	9337	,,	Do.,	do.	do. and do.
	9658	,,	Do.,	do.	Ballytrammy, ...
	9373	,,	Daniel Allen,	Mrs. K. J. Baird,	Drumalad, ...
	9374	,,	John Corkter,	do.	do.
	9373	,,	Thomas Fleming,	do.	do.
	95.62	,,	Andrew Thompson, ...	Marquis of Hertford, ...	Claremore,
					Total, —

COUNTY OF

Assistant Commissioners—					
J. H. Ross (Legal). M. S. PATTERSON. J. G. S. MACBRIDE.	11970	March 9.	Owen Walters,	Mrs. Margaret O'Hagan,	Clonalig
	11938	,,	Mary Rowland,	Alexander F. Towoole and anor., Trustees of T. P. Ball, continued by Horace Thorp, Surviving Trustee.	Urkin,
	11911	,,	Patrick Duffy,	do.	Tan,
	11919	,,	Michael Daly,	Michael J. Kelly,	Carran,
	11180	,,	Anne Gartlan,	do.	Drumboy,
	11190	,,	Anne M'Voy, Ltd. Admix. of Bridget M'Voy.	Alexander K. Synge,	Tullynrod
	11369	,,	Edward Mashen,	do.	do.
	11185	,,	Michael Larman (James).	do.	do.
	11167	,,	Anne Gaurin,	do.,	do.
	11166	,,	Patrick Grimmey,	do.	do.
	11161	,,	Samuel Brown,	do.	Corgalmore,
	11170	,,	Anne Harvey,	Mrs. Margaret O'Hagan,	Clonalig

ULSTER.

ANTRIM.

Land of Holding. Acres.	Poor Law Valuation.	Former Rent.	Judicial Rent.	Observations.	Value of Tenancy.
A. R. P.	£ s. d.	£ s. d.	£ s. d.		£ s. d.
1 0 0	1 5 0	2 15 0	1 8 0		
65 0 14	20 15 0	24 19 0	20 10 0		
1 1 33	—	3 4 6	1 16 0		
20 1 1	—	13 15 6	13 0 0		
47 3 37	15 0 0	13 13 0	13 0 0		
73 1 0	8 2 0	10 15 3	8 0 0		
19 3 5	13 0 0	10 0 0	8 15 0		
1 0 0	unascertained.	1 0 0	0 15 0		
143 0 1	66 5 0	80 5 3	65 4 0		

ARMAGH.

9 1 36	5 10 0	4 16 0	6 1 1		
73 3 30	12 10 0	9 13 0	7 7 9		
7 6 25	4 0 0	8 5 0	2 9 10		
9 1 37	7 0 0	4 5 0	3 8 6		
9 3 35	6 8 0	5 7 2	4 3 0		
6 3 31	4 10 0	4 6 0	6 0 6		
14 0 60	12 10 0	9 11 4	7 10 0		
11 2 14	8 0 0	6 13 0	5 3 3		
17 0 16	9 0 0	6 1 0	4 9 6		
7 3 3	6 0 0	4 17 0	3 7 6		
11 3 33	4 15 0	5 1 0	2 5 9		
77 1 33	14 0 0	13 1 3	8 15 2		

FIRST STATUTORY TERM.

COUNTY OF

Names of Assistant Commissioners by whom Cases were decided.	Record Number.	Date of Order.	Name of Tenant	Name of Landlord	Townland
Assistant Commissioners—		1882.			
W. J. BAILEY (Legal). A. BREMALL, J. MacKENZIE.	11328	March 10,	Richard Wetherall, —	Mrs. A. O. Craig, —	Feybeg, —
	11320	,,	Do., —	do. —	do. —
	11340	„	William Gamble, —	Duke of Abercorn and another, Trees of the Duke of Manchester.	Attiagh, —
					Total.

COUNTY OF

Assistant Commissioners—	7446	Feb. 5,	John Ford,	Major Henry C. Maxwell,	List of, —
J. H. ROSS (Legal). W O'CALLAGHAN. L. CHENEY.	7478	March 17,	James Brady, —	Rev. F Fitzpatrick, —	Thorlabeda,
	7482	„	Patrick Quinn, —	Earl of Lanesborough, —	Kilroosy,
	7483	„	Francis Jerwyn, —	do. —	Drumleesten,
	7463	„	Joseph Dobbs, —	do. —	Aughnadrumgollia,
	7478	„	Charles Reilly, —	do. —	Drumleesten,
	7465	„	Francis Jerwyn, —	do. —	do. —
	7481	„	James Masterson, —	George D. Beresford, D.L.	do. —
	7164	„	Anthony Fitzpatrick,	Col. Sir F. J. Hort, —	Faharlagh, —
	7468	„	Abraham Storey, —	Mrs. Catherine M. Jones,	Drumarno, —
	7470	„	Thomas Smith, —	James H. M. Garrett, —	Lisnoon, —
M. T. GRAAN (Legal). J. D. BOYD. L. CHENEY.	7428	Feb. 24,	Thomas Best, —	Gerald F. Holmes and ors.	Claraflow, —
	7434	„	John Gould, —	The Right Hon. the Earl of Lanesborough.	Quinsy, —
					Total.

COUNTY OF

Assistant Commissioners—	13735	March 2,	Elizabeth Hunter Adnpln. of G. L. Hunter.	Rev. Charles Fawcett.	Glennan Iskh. —
D. TURNEY (Legal). G. H. MILLER. J. W. REMMIT.	13640	March 9,	Robert A. Kane, —	John Scott, —	Carnarvogh, —
	13604	„	Roger Doheny, —	William R. Harte, —	Ardmulin, —
G. N. TERLINE (Legal). R. H. PRINGLE. J. A. SMITH.	13176	Jan. 5,	John Peoples, —	Alexander Black, —	Killymore, —
	13178	March 29,	Daniel McGrath, —	Mrs. Jessie Trench, —	Cavaghmore, —
	13177	„	Robert Lowper, —	do. —	do. —

FIRST STATUTORY TERM.

ARMAGH—continued.

Area of Holding.	Poor Law Valuation.	Former Rent.	Judicial Rent.	Observations.	Value of Tenancy.
A. R. P.	£ s. d.	£ s. d.	£ s. d.		£ s. d.
31 1 20	10 10 0	9 17 5	8 15 0		
6 1 0	6 5 0	5 10 0	3 8 0		
5 1 32	—	5 5 5	1 15 4		
171 3 23	109 13 0	85 10 2	66 13 9		

CAVAN.

31 2 63	6 0 0	5 10 0	5 5 0	By consent.	
8 3 3	6 15 0	5 5 0	4 4 0		
8 3 20	5 13 0	5 0 0	4 4 0		
16 0 10	unascertained,	17 13 8	13 0 0		
19 1 13	16 6 0	16 1 0	10 0 0		
6 1 1	6 5 0	7 14 6	6 0 0		
9 0 85	6 0 0	5 18 4	5 19 4		
26 0 28	17 16 0	16 8 0	11 0 0		
29 1 53	13 10 0	13 1 6	9 16 0		
16 0 18	8 0 0	7 0 0	5 10 0		
25 0 16	13 15 0	13 0 0	11 5 0		
3 0 73	unascertained,	5 17 0	3 18 0		
25 0 31	13 5 0	9 13 0	7 16 0		
201 1 29	118 15 0	176 11 1	85 1 6		

DONEGAL.

73 3 75	59 5 0	45 19 0	71 0 0	By consent.	
4 1 5	1 5 0	1 1 5	0 17 6		
11 5 80	6 10 0	6 6 0	3 13 0	With quarteridge portion of 10s. for 0s. mountain.	
19 5 80	6 15 0	5 10 0	6 5 0	By consent.	
5 7 36	3 10 0	8 5 0	3 18 3		
25 5 23	17 5 0	15 7 0	13 5 4		

IRISH LAND COMMISSION.

FIRST STATUTORY TERM.

Names of Assistant Commissioners by whom Cases were decided.	Record Number.	Date of Order.	Name of Tenant.	Name of Landlord.	Townland
Assistant Commissioners:—		1897.			
C. H. TATLOW (Legal), R. H. PRESTON, J. A. SMITH.	13561	March 22,	John Martin, ...	Mrs. Jessie Trench ...	Carraghmore, ...
	13601	,,	James Bryson, ...	do. ,, ...	do. ,,
	13575	,,	Jaques Leeper (Frank),	do. ,, ...	do. ,,
	13545	,,	William M'Curdy, ..	do. ,, —	do. ,,
	13554	,,	William Patton, ...	do. ,,, ...	do. ,,
	13603	,,	Jaques Bryson, ...	do. ,, ...	do. ,,
	13597	,,	Denis Boner, ...	do. ,,, ...	Moneham, ,,
	13603	,,	James M'Cleary, ...	do. ,,, ...	Carraghmore, ,,
	13540	,,	John M'Olhenny, ...	do. ... —	Carraghmore, ,,
	13579	,,	John Hannigan, ...	do. ,,, ...	do. ,,
	13580	,,	Catherine M'Kann,	do. ,,, ...	do. ,,
	13641	,,	Andrew Leeper, ...	Marquis Conyngham, ...	Dunarley, ,,
	13563	,,	Matthew Rule, ...	James B. Dolop, ...	Drumlegan, ,,
	13720	,,	James Wisley, ...	do. ,, ...	Mounthall, ,,
	13596	,,	Jaques Kelly, ...	do. ,,, ...	Drumlegan, ,,
	13547	,,	Charles Houston, ..	Sir Samuel H. Hayes, bart,	Monmhhbble, ,,
	13507	,,	Catherine Patton, Ltd. Admtk. of Thomas Patton.	do. ,, ...	Cloghore, ,,
	13586	,,	James Knox, ...	do. ,,, ...	Tonneywerth, ,,
	13560	,,	William Magee, ...	do. ,, ...	Coppys, ,,
	13582	,,	Alexander M'Clean, ...	do. ,, ...	do. ,,
	13578	,,	John Leeper, ...	do. ,, ...	do. ,,
	13715	,,	Thompson Robinson,	do. ,, ...	Mullaghals, ,,
D. TRENCH (Legal), R. SWEDLLE, J. M. KELLY.	13626	March 9,	Daniel M'Maskin, ...	Michael King and others, Trustees of Rev. Thomas M'Clelland, deceased.	Three Tont,
	13526	,,	Richard Rankine, ...	do. ,,,	do. ,,
	13624	,,	Mary M'Cahan, ...	do. ,, ...	do. ,,
	13520	,,	Jaques Anthony, ...	do. ,,, —	do. ,,
	13619	,,	Do. — ...	do. ,, ...	do. ,,
	13618	,,	James Smyth, ...	do. ,,, —	do. ,,
	13617	,,	Edward Doherty, ...	do. ,,, ...	do. ,,
	13614	,,	William Quigley, ...	do. ,,, ...	do. ,,
	13613	,,	James Hughes, ...	do. ,,, —	do. ,,

FIRST STATUTORY TERM.

DONEGAL—continued.

Area of Holding.	Poor Law Valuation.	Former Rent.	Judicial Rent.	Observations.	Value of Tenancy
A. R. P.	£ s. d.	£ s. d.	£ s. d.		£ s. d.
19 1 20	17 6 0	17 10 0	11 16 6		
15 1 03	unascertained.	16 7 5	9 18 1		
25 1 15	11 13 0	10 0 0	8 13 1		
21 3 3	20 0 0	18 10 0	14 0 1		
19 0 03	17 0 0	16 5 0	13 7 2		
17 2 6	unascertained.	10 13 0	5 13 6		
36 3 6	4 10 0	6 0 0	3 11 11		
18 2 25	5 0 0	4 0 0	2 7 1		
122 0 30	23 2 0	19 16 0	17 13 3		
8 3 0	4 5 0	4 5 0	3 17 3		
23 1 31	9 15 0	9 10 0	8 15 6		
1 3 03	3 10 0	2 1 0	0 19 5		
13 3 03	6 10 5	6 13 0	5 19 4		
67 0 0	34 0 0	23 5 9	20 11 11		
15 0 15	6 10 0	6 5 1	5 19 0		
66 1 0	10 0 0	10 0 0	7 7 3		
30 0 0	4 10 0	5 0 0	8 16 5		
62 3 26	21 15 0	21 10 5	13 7 5		
47 0 0	13 5 0	12 17 4	10 5 9		
17 3 0	6 10 0	6 0 0	5 5 0		
1 3 16	3 0 0	3 5 9	2 5 9		
64 5 03	7 5 0	5 10 0	5 7 6		
34 0 0	14 0 0	13 0 0	9 0 0		
21 3 0	16 15 0	11 0 0	8 13 0		
7 3 03	4 0 0	6 3 0	3 13 0	With an undivided 1-5th of 3a. 3r. 2p. and an undivided 1-5th of 3a. 0r. 14p.	
3 5 03	5 0 0	4 3 0	3 10 0		
13 3 0	5 5 0	4 15 0	3 15 0		
11 3 0	7 0 0	6 0 0	4 0 0		
14 0 6	4 6 0	4 3 6	3 0 0		
38 0 0	23 10 0	21 13 5	15 10 0		
29 0 26	11 13 0	10 3 0	7 10 0		

IRISH LAND COMMISSION.

FIRST STATUTORY TERM.

COUNTY OF

Names of Assistant Commissioners by whom Cases were decided.	Record Number.	Date of Order.	Name of Tenant.	Name of Landlord.	Townland.
Assistant Commissioners—		1887.			
D. Tuohy (Legal). R. Sproule. J. M. Kelly.	13608	March 9,	Patrick M'Cullion,	Michael King and others, Trustees of Rev. Thomas M'Clelland, deceased.	Three Dens
	13607	„	Denis M'Cullion,	do.	do.
	13606	„	Mary M'Cullion,	do.	do.
	13591	„	Thomas M'Nally,	do.	do.
	13534	„	Aaron Beck,	Robert J. Beck,	Kildrum
	13513	„	John E. Welsh,	Thomas Keogh and others, Executors of Thomas Newman, deceased.	Fegary,
	13574	„	Do.,	do.	do.
	13573	„	Henry O.R.	Jas. F. Wallace & another,	Maurragh,
	13636	„	Henry Frizzell,	Michael King and others, Trustees of Rev. Thomas M'Clelland.	Ballingate,
					Teal,

COUNTY OF

Assistant Commissioners—	13024	March 5,	James Lynaby,	Captain Roger Hall,	Ballygorgan
W. P. Baker (Legal). G. W. Thompson. D. O'C. Donellan.	13078	„	Thomas Ennis,	Captain John Harrison,	Kirkinan,
	13011	„	John Ennis (Todd),	do.	do.
	13056	„	Mary Falconer,	do.	Ballywood,
	13052	„	Wm. M'Caffrey and another,	do.	Ballynamman
	13048	„	Samuel Vance,	do.	Ballyteerigan
	13162	„	William Ennis,	do.	Kirkinan,
	13073	„	Daniel Bennett,	Hugh Clelland,	Castleboy,
	13414	March 22,	Hugh Quinn,	Earl of Kilmurry,	Coyfell,
	12874	„	Joseph M'Rithin,	do.	Maquillsmote
	13110	March 24,	Patrick O'Hara,	Earl of Annesley,	Ballyangrim
	12866	„	Bernard Flinn & others,	do.	Ballyndary,
	12860	„	Thomas Hay,	Francis Hayes,	Teys,
	12143	„	Thomas Holland,	Capt. R. M'G. R. Sholton,	Ballyteran
	12090	„	Do.,	do.	do.
	12088	„	Do.,	do.	do.
	12614	„	James Murphy,	General Wm. Montresor,	Ballymowr,
	12611	„	Nicholas Davidson,	C. K. Cordner & another,	Ballynamman
	12560	„	Do.,	do.	do.

FIRST STATUTORY TERM.

DONEGAL —continued.

Area of Holding.	Poor Law Valuation.	Former Rent.	Judicial Rent.	Observations.	Value of Tenancy.
A. R. P.	£ s. d.	£ s. d.	£ s. d.		£ s. d.
11 0 24		6 19 0	6 0 0		
31 0 34	11 10 0	5 18 0	5 0 0		
11 0 34		5 19 0	4 2 0		
43 0 30	80 10 0	43 0 0	34 5 5		
30 3 25	63 10 0	71 6 4	43 16 0		
13 1 0	4 10 0	3 0 0	2 15 0		
3 3 30	3 3 0	5 0 0	1 16 0		
40 1 27	3 10 0	4 16 0	3 10 0		
11 0 0	3 10 0	3 16 0	2 17 0		
579 1 7	585 1 5	561 16 11	419 3 3		

DOWN.

6 1 0	3 5 0	7 0 0	5 16 0		
15 3 30	23 0 0	15 10 0	10 6 0		
7 0 33	3 10 0	6 7 6	4 6 4		
17 0 31	30 15 0	24 0 0	15 15 0		
5 3 38	7 10 0	6 1 0	3 15 0		
31 3 00	24 1 0	20 0 0	18 17 4		
9 9 33	6 3 0	7 13 0	5 0 0		
3 3 34	3 5 0	3 4 1	2 4 0		
14 3 30	19 0 0	14 4 3	11 10 0	By consent.
31 0 37	18 0 0	14 15 3	11 0 0	do.
7 3 33	2 10 0	3 5 0	2 5 0		
3 1 33	4 0 0	4 0 0	3 10 0		
3 3 30	6 0 0	7 0 0	4 3 6		
33 0 24	21 5 0	18 0 0	18 3 0		
31 0 0	31 0 0	21 0 0	13 10 0		
15 0 0	31 0 0	17 15 6	13 4 0		
44 3 23	47 5 0	45 0 0	31 3 0		
1 0 3	unmeasured.	1 7 10	0 14 0		
6 3 27	do.	7 5 0	4 15 0		

IRISH LAND COMMISSION.

FIRST STATUTORY TERM.

Names of Assistant Commissioners by whom Cases were decided.	Record Number.	Date of Order.	Name of Tenant.	Name of Landlord.	Townland.
Assistant Commissioners—		1887.			
W. F. Bailey (Legal). W. H. O. Eyre. J. Armstrong.	12097	Mar. 26,	John Wallace Shaw, ...	Ralph J. Hunter & others, Trustees of Gen. J. Hunter	Orreny, —
W. F. Bailey (Legal). G. Byrne. I. G. Williams.	12157	Mar. 14,	J. Young and another,	James Birch, — ...	Ballymeny, —
	17160	„	John Munroe, ...	do. ...	do.
	18159	„	Thomas Quinn & anr.	do. ...	do.
	12155	„	Joseph Young & anr.	do. ...	do.
	19135	„	Robert M'Cracken, —	Mrs. Ellen Carton & anr.	McRedcroplet,
	12185	„	Agnes Arnold, ...	do. ...	do.
	12163	„	John Law, ...	do. ...	do.
	18157	„	Mary Craig, — ...	do. ...	do.
	12163	„	Charles M'Crady, —	Rev. Edward Hackstan, Trus. of John Prathleton,	Magheralin, —
					Total.

Assistant Commissioners—	5703	Feb. 27,	Christopher Willis, —	Lord Lanesboro' ...	Kilford,
A. R. Mortemckley. A. A. Drane.	5834	„	John Pervis, — ...	George Members, ...	Lisduff,
	5897	„	Catherine M'Kervey,	Thomas Magwire, —	Edenduo Cast.
	5593	„	John Gannie, —	Augustin Archdale & others,	Dromnain.
	5472	„	William Gannie, —	do. —	do.
	5691	„	Thomas Uenain, —	do. — ...	do.
	6549	„	James Carson & anr.	John Beatty and another,	Drummeil
	5973	„	Robert Wauen, —	John Armstrong and tenr.	Edgartenings
	5640	„	William Cunningham.	Upton Moreney, ...	Clonakilpin.
C. H. Fleming (Legal). H. Johnston. O. M'Elligott.	5703	Mar. 31,	William Jones, ...	H. M. Campbell and anr.	Garrigorm.
	5703	Jan. 31,	William Praw, — ...	do. —	McEnghmm.
	5704	Mar. 22,	W. O. Winslow, —	H. N. Latimer, —	Clogher & anr.
	5761	„	Francis Graham, —	A. P. Heywood-Lonsdale,	Tullinheny.
	5703	„	Robert Platt, —	do. — ...	Quinnagh —
	5720	„	Robert Hamilton, —	do. —	Pattinbry.

FIRST STATUTORY TERM.

DOWN—*continued.*

Area of Holding. Statute	Poor Law Valuation.	Former Rent.	Judicial Rent.	Observations.	Value of Tenancy.
A. R. P.	£ s. d.	£ s. d.	£ s. d.		£ s. d.
20 0 0	27 0 0	28 0 0	24 10 0		
11 3 23	11 5 0	11 11 6	8 15 0		
5 0 0	6 5 0	6 9 0	3 13 6		
13 0 30	13 13 0	11 3 6	8 17 8		
13 3 10	13 10 0	11 17 3	8 8 0		
5 3 0	7 10 0	6 0 6	4 6 0		
3 3 30	6 0 0	8 8 0	8 12 6		
9 1 18	10 0 0	9 6 6	7 7 0		
17 8 20	8 19 0	17 5 6	19 7 6		
3 1 0	3 10 0	3 6 6	8 10 0		
738 8 23	827 0 0	380 17 9	250 15 0		

FERMANAGH

24 3 10	24 0 0	23 3 6	16 7 0		
21 0 9	19 10 0	19 10 0	18 10 0		
8 0 0	6 8 0	5 18 0	4 8 0		
16 3 10	11 0 0	11 15 0	8 0 0		
20 3 0	24 0 0	23 17 6	16 13 0		
15 3 10	16 10 0	11 16 0	6 15 0		
33 0 0	25 5 0	27 0 0	16 5 0		
7 2 12	6 15 0	6 8 0	6 7 0		
23 0 23	17 0 0	15 14 0	13 10 0		
16 1 23	10 0 0	8 10 0	6 10 0		
15 0 14	11 0 0	10 10 0	8 0 0	By consent
50 0 83	81 0 0	31 0 8	81 0 0		
8 5 0	5 15 0	4 1 6	8 2 8		
1 0 10	3 10 0	1 11 10	0 14 6		
3 8 15	6 10 0	7 0 6	3 15 0		

MAR C 2

IRISH LAND COMMISSION.

FIRST STATUTORY TERM.

Names of Assistant Commissioners by whom Cases were decided.	Record Number.	Date of Order.	Name of Tenant.	Name of Landlord.	Townland.
Assistant Commissioners—		1887.			
C. H. Teeling (Legal). H. Johnston. G. M'Elliott.	5784	March 23,	Robert Flack, —	A. P. Heywood Lonsdale,	Cashryaugh,
	5786	„	Barham Montgomery,	Robert Moore and another,	Aughinloo,
	5782	„	Peter Krish, ...	Governors of Vaughan's Charity School.	Carnsore,
C. H. Teeling (Legal). A. S. Drape. R. J. Crane.	5716	„	Ellen Fallon, ...	Commissioners of Education in Ireland.	Derrytrah,
	5718	„	James Murphy,	do. ... —	Drumbranghan,
	5714	„	Thomas M'Manus, ..	do. — ...	Anniagh West,
	5712	„	John Boyle, ...	do. — ...	Drumbargy,
	5711	„	Michael Boyle, —	do. ... —	do.
	5718	„	Hugh Corrigan, —	do. ... —	Rowantrey,
	5719	„	Henry Cox, —	Christopher Wilson, ...	Shan,
	5793	„	Charles Lenny, ...	Mrs. Annie Adams, ...	Cloghambly,
	5141	„	John M'Caffrey,	Rev. William Hall & others,	Drumgallon,
	5770	„	James Grey, ...	J. W. Richards, —	Drummiskin, ...
	5765	„	John Brown, ...	Mrs Wilhelmina Braddell,	Lapland, ..
	5400	„	John Cregg, surid. in name of Rose Cregg,	Dr. Christopher Hunter & another,	Cartowhill,
	5192	„	Andrew M'Manus, ...	John de Irwin, ...	Rammen & son
	5745	„	Ellen Price & another,	Mrs Graham Bailey, —	Inniskian,
	5736	„	John Irvine, ...	Earl of Enniskillen, ...	Derrygoodall,
	5799	„	Andrew Thompson, ...	do. ...	Drumcoolmcnagher
	5798	„	Henry Barton, ...	do. ...	Killydrain,
	5760	„	Bridget Dolan, ...	do. ...	Corcluntowry,
	5712	„	Hugh Corrigan, junior,	Commissioners of Education in Ireland.	Rowantrey,
	5716	„	Thomas M'Manus, ...	do. —	Anniagh West,
	5717	„	Richard Corrigan, ...	do. ... —	Drumbraghan
	5740	„	James Maguire, ...	do.	Rowantrey,
	5787	„	Bernard Maskell, ...	do.	Drumbraghan
	5572	„	Nathaniel Corrigan,	do.	Rowantrey,
	5575	„	Francis M'Manus, ...	do.	Drumbraghan
	5739	„	John M'Manus, ...	do.	do.
	5545	„	Rev. Pat. M'Gowran,	do.	Drumard
	5772	„	Bernard Maskell, ...	do.	Drumbraghan
	5573	„	Andrew M'Caffrey, ...	do.	do.

FIRST STATUTORY TERM.

FERMANAGH—*continued.*

Description of Holding—Quality	Poor Law Valuation	Former Rent	Judicial Rent	Observations	Value of Tenancy
A. R. P.	£ s. d.	£ s. d.	£ s. d.		£ s. d.
9 2 5	10 0 0	10 0 0	7 5 0		
71 3 13	15 10 0	12 2 11	8 3 6		
19 1 38	7 15 0	9 10 0	5 10 0		
19 0 15	13 0 0	11 10 3	6 12 0		
19 2 7	8 15 0	7 14 2	5 13 0		
12 1 50	7 10 0	8 11 11	8 0 0		
9 0 30	4 8 0	5 13 8	6 0 0		
11 1 14	6 10 0	7 10 1	8 0 0		
9 3 31	7 10 0	6 4 3½	5 13 0		
1 2 30	0 13 0	3 0 0	3 0 0		
17 1 30	13 0 0	15 8 0	9 17 0		
38 8 19	19 10 0	17 0 0	11 14 0		
13 3 30	8 10 0	8 1 8	8 0 0		
90 0 10	47 15 0	48 0 0	37 0 0		
5 0 23	1 10 0	3 15 0	3 1 6		
15 1 11	19 8 0	21 0 0	15 5 0		
13 0 30	11 10 0	11 7 8	8 0 0		
12 2 0	3 15 0	4 4 0	8 0 0		
8 0 15	4 0 0	5 15 0	3 0 0		
13 0 23	6 17 0	8 17 6	4 15 0		
8 3 10	8 15 0	4 13 0	4 0 0		
5 2 80	5 0 8	4 0 0	8 11 0		
4 2 35	4 0 0	3 17 4	2 10 0		
20 1 15	16 5 0	11 8 11	7 19 0		
11 3 30	8 0 0	7 13 9	3 10 0		
11 1 80	7 8 0	7 18 3	5 16 0		
7 3 35	8 0 0	7 8 8	5 5 0		
11 1 30	5 0 0	8 15 8	3 13 8		
13 0 1	16 3 0	8 9 3	7 5 0		
11 0 30	7 0 0	7 10 0	4 0 0		
8 3 7	8 0 0	3 13 8	3 5 0		
85 3 0	13 0 0	8 17 6	5 8 0		

IRISH LAND COMMISSION.

FIRST STATUTORY TERM.

COUNTY OF

Names of Assistant Commissioners by whom Cases were decided.	Record Number.	Date of Order.	Name of Tenant.	Name of Landlord.	Townland.
Assistant Commissioners —		1897.			
G. H. THELAND (Legal). A. S. DEANE. E. J. GRANT.	5742	March 23,	Patrick Maguire, —	Commissioners of Education in Ireland.	Mullans, &c.
	5710	"	Hugh Corrigan, —	do. — —	Ramsleny, "
	5725	"	John Maskell, —	do. — —	do. "
	5727	"	John Corrigan, —	do. — —	Derrylaveloght,
	5710	"	James Ballour, —	do. — —	Drumlargy,
	5701	"	Maurice Owens, —	do. — —	Sesslagh.
	5725	"	Patrick Drogan, —	do. — —	Drumbroughan.
	5742	"	Patrick McManus, —	do. — —	Sesslagh.
	5774	"	Thomas Maguire, —	do. — —	Ramsleny.
	5725	"	Mary Murray, —	do. — —	Drumbroughan.
					Total.

COUNTY OF

Assistant Commissioners —	5364	March 8,	Robert Campbell, —	Joseph Christie,	Tawnry,
D. TUCKEY (Legal). R. HEWSON. J. M. KELLY.	5465	"	William Donnell, —	do. —	do.
	5444	"	Edward Lynch, —	George Knox, —	Dunlough.
	5417	"	Martin McChesley, —	Joseph S. McCrecheen, —	Monaghan.
	5346	"	Matthew Stevenson, —	Charles Davidson, —	Null.
	5297	"	Nancy McGillesbey, —	Rem. Stephen Montgomery de la Poer Horsenford, —	Garvenisgagh.
	5384	"	John Gormley, —	do. —	Cattmanagh.
	5325	"	John Harron, —	Captain R. B. Stothert, —	Killinchugel.
	5339	"	David Thompson, —	George Tomkins, —	Mahony.
					Total.

FIRST STATUTORY TERM.

FERMANAGH —continued.

Extent of Holding. Acres.	Poor Law Valuation.	Former Rent.	Judicial Rent.	Observations.	Value of Tenancy.
A. R. P.	£ s. d.	£ s. d.	£ s. d.		£ s. d.
7 3 16	6 0 0	4 11 3	3 16 0		
16 1 25	13 0 0	10 11 1½	8 0 0		
30 0 25	8 4 0	6 17 3	6 0 0		
13 3 23	7 6 0	6 9 6	3 5 0		
11 3 25	16 0 6	3 9 6	7 0 0		
15 3 2	10 6 9	8 2 11	7 16 0		
13 3 10	6 15 0	5 14 11	6 5 0		
17 1 0	11 5 5	8 7 6	6 10 0		
19 1 10	16 6 0	14 1 0	11 10 0		
8 0 33	4 3 0	6 6 6	3 0 0		
923 5 95	433 13 0	343 10 3	119 6 6		

LONDONDERRY.

16 1 25	17 16 0	13 0 0	9 16 0		
11 3 0	7 10 0	10 10 0	5 10 0		
3 1 30	8 15 0	4 15 0	3 10 0		
13 3 10	1Y 0 0	18 0 0	13 10 0		
7 0 0	16 0 0	16 0 0	6 16 0		
34 0 0	8 0 0	9 0 0	5 6 0		
36 0 16	9 13 0	9 13 6	7 0 0		
19 3 13	15 5 6	12 13 0	6 16 0		
11 1 10	10 10 6	18 6 0	6 16 0		
115 3 17	106 7 0	104 18 0	71 6 6		

MONAGHAN.

FIRST STATUTORY TERM.

COUNTY OF

Names of Assistant Commissioners by whom cases were decided	Record Number	Date of Order	Name of Tenant	Name of Landlord		Townland
Assistant Commissioners—		1887.				
J. H. Ross (Legal). R. A. G. Adamson. W. Jephott.	5300	March 5,	Mary Kairney, ...	Lord Rossmore,	—	Donakey,
	5291	„	Thomas Carey Shartey,	do. —	...	Kildorolly,
	5299	„	Eliza M'Cabe, ...	do. ...	—	Kagurragh,
	5294	„	Samuel Adams, ...	R. T. Bernard,	...	Corlott,
	5313	March 13,	Joseph Miller. ...	Sir John Leslie, Bart.,	—	Drummav,
	5317	„	William M'Cradden,	do. ...	—	do.
	5316	„	James M'Cullough, —	do. ...	—	do.
	5304	„	Robert Hay, —	do. ...	—	do.
						Total, —

COUNTY OF

Names of Assistant Commissioners	Record Number	Date of Order	Name of Tenant	Name of Landlord		Townland
Assistant Commissioners—	12940	Feb. 27,	Daniel M'Gurk, ...	Rev. A. R. Irwin,	—	Derraghadun,
J. M. Teevan (Legal). J. Hovlen. W. Small.	12845	„	Owen M'Mahon, —	do. ...	...	Kellybunchy,
	12843	„	Eliza Reynolds, ...	do. —	—	Derraghadun & another,
	12847	„	John Kelly, ...	do. —	—	Derraghadun, —
C. H. Teeling (Legal). W. A. Mewe.	12524	March 20,	James Hemphill. ...	Duke of Abercorn,	...	Tullywhim, —
	12528	„	Samuel M'Corkell. ..	Earl of Erne, —	—	Lifford Common & another,
C. H. Teeling (Legal). R. Jacobson. G. M'Elliott.	12940	March 12,	James Ingram, ...	Geo. C. Landrum,	—	Drummuck,
	12941	„	Edward Woods, ...	do. —	—	do.
	12931	„	William Morris, ...	do. ...	...	Scaben,
	12937	„	Charles O'Donnell, ...	William D. Irvine,	—	Lettergub, —
G. H. Caldwell. J. Hovlen.	12515	March 5,	James M'Kinney, —	Elizabeth J. M'Combard & others,		Cloughfin,
	12510	„	Rose Kelly, —	do. —	—	do.
	12523	„	Oliver Crawford, —	John T. Galbraith,	—	Dunkirem,
	12873	„	Thomas M'Coy, ..	Earl of Belmore,	—	Rakeepa,
	18703	„	Francis Owens, ...	do. ...	—	Durm,
	18708	„	Do. ...	do. ...	—	do.
						Total,

FIRST STATUTORY TERM.

MONAGHAN—continued.

Extent of Holding. Plantn.	Poor Law Valuation.	Former Rent.	Judicial Rent.	Observations.	Value of Tenancy.
A. R. P.	£ s. d.	£ s. d.	£ s. d.		£ s. d.
20 0 25	12 0 0	12 10 0	9 2 0		
13 0 10	12 10 0	12 10 0	9 3 0		
10 1 20	8 3 0	7 10 0	9 4 0		
13 0 20	14 0 0	13 0 0	8 10 0		
25 0 29	23 10 0	21 0 4	14 5 0		
19 0 21	17 10 0	16 3 0	9 10 0		
8 3 32	8 8 0	5 19 1	4 14 0		
20 0 22	23 10 0	18 0 0	22 0 0		
172 1 1	174 5 0	171 4 3	118 1 0		

TYRONE.

0 1 63	3 8 0	3 10 0	8 9 0		
7 3 10	0 19 0	6 0 0	4 13 2		
6 0 8	3 0 0	0 11 4	3 13 0		
0 3 11	5 10 0	7 0 0	5 9 1		
60 0 27	33 10 0	29 8 8	22 10 0		
38 1 30	30 10 0	35 14 0	77 3 4		
25 0 8	18 6 0	10 6 0	16 0 0		
18 1 22	13 5 0	13 0 0	11 0 0		
28 0 18	18 10 0	15 5 0	14 10 0		
17 1 11	10 0 0	10 0 0	9 0 0		
24 2 17	14 10 0	13 0 0	10 0 0		
8 0 20	5 5 0	5 0 0	4 4 0		
12 8 0	8 5 0	10 0 0	8 7 8		
28 3 0	15 5 0	17 0 0	9 10 0		
14 0 10	40 15 0	45 16 0	50 10 0		
11 1 30	37 0 0	29 0 0	20 18 0		

FIRST STATUTORY TERM.

PROVINCE OF

COUNTY OF

Names of Assistant Commissioners by whom Cases were decided	Record Number	Date of Order	Name of Tenant	Name of Landlord	Townland
Assistant Commissioners— L. Doyle (Legal). A. N. Coyne. G. R. Bolster.		1897.			
	1651	May. 30,	Thomas Seaver,	H. D. Nisbsb,	Rathkennory,
	1650	″	Joseph Rogers,	do.	do.
	1647	″	Patrick Farrell,	H. Owen Lewis,	Snakers West,
	1640	″	Thomas Kennedy,	General John Davis,	Newtown,
	1635	″	Myles Quinn,	James J. Robinson,	Aughfarrell,
	1537	″	William Carr,	Lord Annaly,	Bracknistown,
	1648	″	John Rogers,	Lord Langford,	Ballywinters,
	1672	″	Do.	do.	Tubber,
	1646	″	Mary Agnes Bell,	do.	do.
	1643	″	Do.	do.	do.
	1648	″	William Dowdall,	Sarah Kelly,	Carrigan,
	1631	″	Patrick Brennan,	Mr. A. A. Gunn,	Finglas,
	1644	″	Bernard Atlee,	Barnum Annaly,	Barbarsstown,
	1659	″	Thomas Thornton,	Rt. Hon. J. T. Hamilton,	Milverton,
	1630	″	Matthew Reid,	Lt.-Col. W. J. Alexander,	Gortinrush and
	1633	Feb. 4,	Patrick Darton,	Rt. Hon. Leo T. Hamilton,	Ballinasloe & way
	1659	″	Do	do.	Toorspola,
	1691	Mar. 10,	Pierce Reynolds and another	Lieut.-Col. Alexander,	Newtown,
	1656	″	Christopher Healy,	Rt. Hon. Leo T. Hamilton,	Florence,
	1645	″	Do.	do.	Holmpatrick,
	1637	″	Do.	do.	Toorspola,
	1673	″	Patrick Flanagan,	do.	Milverton,
	1687	″	Thomas Thornton,	do.	Loughlush,
	1664	″	Joseph Grimley,	do.	Milverton,
	1660	″	John Dowling,	do.	do.
	1664	″	Fox Healy, credit in name of James Healy.	do.	do.
	1631	″	James Gowan,	do.	Toorspola

LEINSTER.

DUBLIN.

Quant. of Holdings.	Poor Law Valuation.	Former Rent.	Judicial Rent.	Observations.	Value of Tenancy.
A. R. P.	£ s. d.	£ s. d.	£ s. d.		£ s. d.
17 0 38	13 15 0	16 0 0	12 10 0		
3 1 6	8 5 0	8 18 0	8 16 0		
5 1 37	8 15 0	15 0 0	11 15 0		
9 3 25	17 10 0	17 10 0	14 0 0		
140 2 6	43 0 0	40 0 0	38 0 0		
15 3 17	25 0 0	21 3 11	17 0 0		
2 0 6	8 10 0	3 11 5	3 3 0		
6 0 1	7 15 0	7 15 3	8 8 8		
16 0 35	18 0 0	20 12 0	13 10 0		
3 2 28	5 0 0	8 1 5	7 9 0		
4 0 3	10 15 0	12 0 0	9 0 0		
3 1 0	6 3 0	6 0 0	7 0 0		
144 1 29	154 0 0	323 10 0	172 0 0		
26 3 13	21 15 0	20 15 0	20 15 0		
10 0 20	—	13 5 0	11 7 0	By amount.	
16 3 15	16 15 0	25 7 8	18 0 0	do.	
25 2 16	23 15 0	31 17 8	27 0 0	do.	
810 1 6	234 0 0	233 8 0	238 5 0		
13 0 34	14 0 0	20 15 0	16 0 0		
18 0 7	30 0 0	34 4 5	22 0 0		
4 0 15	8 15 0	13 7 8	9 0 0		
11 3 6	11 6 0	22 15 4	14 19 6		
8 3 0	10 0 0	11 6 7	9 10 0		
6 3 4	8 15 0	6 9 3	6 0 0		
17 5 9	11 10 0	17 15 9	14 0 0		
38 0 34	77 0 0	80 3 10	70 0 0		
11 3 73	16 5 0	18 10 10	15 10 0		

MAR.

IRISH LAND COMMISSION.

FIRST STATUTORY TERM.

Names of Assistant Commissioners by whom Case was decided.	Record Number.	Date of Order.	Name of Tenant.	Name of Landlord.	Townland.
Assistant Commissioners—		1897.			
L. Doyle (Legal). A. M. Couve. G. S. Bolster.	1673	March 30,	Patrick Murtagh,	Rt. Hon. Ion T. Hamilton,	Baltrasna,
	1670	„	Do.,	do.,	Drewparks,
	1648	„	Nicholas Durkan,	do.,	Barnaquenagh,
	1485	„	Do.,	do.,	Town parks,
	1642	„	Do.,	do.,	do.,
	1649	„	Joseph M'Nally,	do.,	do.,
	1655	„	Bridget Ramsey, Ltd. Administration of Allen Ramsey.	Sir R. W. H. Palmer, Bart.,	Dereytown,
					Total,

Assistant Commissioners—	1105	Feb. 24,	James Quinn,	Earl of Longford,	Coolamey,
M. T. Creas (Legal). J. D. Boyle. L. Curran.	3239	„	John Campbell,	Alicia Arthur, Constance Arthur, and Mabelle Arthur, Minors, by G. F. Baker, their Guardian, and Lilian V. Smyth and Gertrude M. Smyth, Minors, by Matthew Smyth, their Guardian.	Rosda 2,
	3127	„	Denis Canavan,	Mrs. Marian O'Weston,	Ballyduff,
	3223	„	Francis Small,	Scottish Provident Institution.	Cloonagher,
					Total,

Assistant Commissioners—	3672	March 17,	John Kennan,	Lord Castletown,	Gash,
M. T. Creas (Legal). F. M. Gaskell. J. Hawkins.	3560	„	James Roberts,	Lord Carbery,	Garlingstown,
	3643	„	Michael Keogh,	Mrs. Francis Bowles,	Cloonelluen,
	3348	„	Maurice Healy,	Countess Wittgenstein,	Knapton,
	3669	„	Daniel Quan,	Viscount De Vesci,	Rathmoy's
	3370	„	Do.,	do.,	Ballynahinch,
	3377	„	James Phelan,	David B. Jacob,	Linds,
	3376	„	Maria Phelan,	do.,	do.,
	3679	„	Catherine Delaney,	do.,	do.,
					Total,

FIRST STATUTORY TERM.

DUBLIN—continued.

Area of Holding	Poor Law Valuation	Former Rent	Judicial Rent	Observations	Term of Survey
A. R. P.	£ s. d.	£ s. d.	£ s. d.		£ s. d.
27 1 39	19 0 0	31 13 0	27 10 0		
5 1 10	3 16 0	6 15 0	3 10 0		
15 3 30	16 0 0	16 16 6	16 12 3		
11 0 1	13 10 0	20 8 6	14 10 0		
6 3 10	8 16 0	17 10 2	8 10 0		
11 0 25	17 10 0	30 13 3	16 0 0		
8 3 16	9 10 0	13 16 0	10 9 0		
464 3 30	570 0 0	1,142 12 10	997 16 4		

LONGFORD.

19 1 25	16 0 0	21 0 0	19 0 0		
14 0 0	7 10 0	7 10 0	5 4 0		
14 3 11	10 10 0	10 6 7	7 15 0		
21 1 14	13 0 0	13 18 3	10 18 0		
75 1 10	48 5 0	62 11 9	43 16 0		

COUNTY.

9 1 6	6 5 0	7 0 0	6 7 0		
16 1 7	8 15 0	6 10 0	6 0 0		
133 1 3	65 10 0	60 0 0	72 10 0		
20 2 36	13 5 0	18 11 0	11 5 0		
3 3 33	3 6 0	6 1 0	3 0 0		
11 3 13	7 10 0	10 16 0	10 13 0		
11 3 0	8 0 0	6 11 2	6 17 6	Form 38.	
3 3 36	8 0 0	6 13 0	5 5 0	do.	
30 0 27	10 0 0	14 11 8	9 7 6	do.	
253 1 31	134 10 0	155 19 2	135 10 0		

IRISH LAND COMMISSION.

FIRST STATUTORY TERM.

Names of Assistant Commissioners by whom Cases were decided.	Record Number.	Date of Order.	Name of Tenant.	Name of Landlord.	Townland.
Assistant Commissioners— M. T. Cahill (Legal). J. D. Boyd. L. Cahill.		1897. Feb. 26,			
	5287	Feb. 26,	Michael Carolan,	Hugh F. Wilson,	Derryn,
	3244	,,	Thomas Morris,	do.	do.
	3245	,,	Edward Reilly,	do.	do.
	3264	,,	Peter Dalton,	do.	do.
	3283	,,	Bryan Dalton,	do.	do.
	3261	,,	Owen Fagan,	do.	do.
	3260	,,	Joseph Darby,	do.	do.
					Total,

Names of Assistant Commissioners	Record No.	Date of Order.	Name of Tenant.	Name of Landlord.	Townland.
Assistant Commissioners— L. Doyle (Legal). O. O'Keeffe. J. Rice.	6854	March 12,	Bridget Kenna,	Robert M. Crowe,	Coberhmore,
	6896	,,	Bartholomew Geoghty,	John F. V. Fitzgerald,	Cabor,
	8708	,,	James Foresman,	Patrick Guthrie,	Knockown,
	8704	,,	Mrs. Margaret Garvey, Limited, Admx. of Stephen Garvey, decd.	Arthur K. Molony,	Clappystown,
	6495	,,	Mrs. Mary Healy,	Henry Twomly,	Curraboe,
	6491	,,	John Considine,	Horan & O'Brien,	Springhall,
	6462	,,	Bridget Quin,	W. R. M'Grath and C. W. H. M'Grath, by Elizabeth M. M'Grath, their mother and Guardian,	Drive,
	8710	,,	Patrick Cudmore,	Col. John O'Callaghan,	Faniowebeg,
	6577	,,	James Nayins,	Alexander K. M'Entire & others, Assignees of Chas. Vyse, deceased,	Caherwalarry,
	6601	,,	Malachy O'Loughlin,	Mary Kenny and another,	Ballyon Beg,
					Total,

Names of Assistant Commissioners	Record No.	Date of Order.	Name of Tenant.	Name of Landlord.	Townland.
Assistant Commissioners— J. Doyle (Legal). S. O. Prior. E. Morrissy.	16558	March 23,	Timothy Murphy,	Walter Noblett, a minor, by Rev. J. W. Noblett, his Guardian and next friend,	Kilbrown,
	19675	,,	Daniel O'Mahony,	Miss S. H. Cummins,	Ballyvoloon,
	16556	,,	Mary Horthy,	Captain D. Connor,	Vinnstown,
	16501	,,	Andrew Mahony,	R. D. Hare,	West Budgretown,

FIRST STATUTORY TERM.

WESTMEATH

Name of Holding, Acres.	Poor Law Valuation.	Former Rent.	Judicial Rent.	Observations.	Value of Tenancy.
A. R. P.	£ s. d.	£ s. d.	£ s. d.		£ s. d.
1 1 30	1 0 0	1 11 0	1 11 0		
10 0 12	5 0 0	8 0 0	5 18 0		
10 3 33	uncertained	1 0 0	1 0 0		
11 9 04	do.	4 13 0	4 0 0		
10 1 53	do.	5 0 0	5 10 0		
15 3 20	do.	5 0 0	4 4 0		
21 1 35	do.	6 0 0	5 5 0		
19 1 33	7 0 0	33 10 0	19 13 0		

MUNSTER.

CLARE.

13 0 15	18 5 0	25 0 0	18 0 0		
13 0 0	13 15 0	17 17 0	11 0 0		
15 1 24	8 15 0	11 0 0	7 3 0		
11 5 17	16 18 0	13 16 0	10 10 0		
19 3 10	14 0 0	13 10 0	16 4 0		
10 5 3	46 0 0	46 17 4	36 10 0		
6 1 1	8 14 0	4 0 0	3 12 4		
4 1 10	8 15 0	4 0 0	2 16 0		
3 1 0	1 0 0	0 15 0	0 10 0		
1 1 19	uncertained	1 0 0	0 5 5		
134 3 17	131 3 0	157 15 8	106 17 0		

CIVIL BILL COURTS.

FIRST STATUTORY TERM.

. COUNTY OF

Names of Assistant Commissioners by whom Courts were holden.	Record Number	Date of Order.	Name of Tenant.	Name of Landlord.	Townland.
Assistant Commissioners—		1897.			
L. Doyle (Legal). E. O. Part.	15610	Mar. 23,	Elizabeth Ahern, —	Robert H. M. Eyre, —	Oranbawn &c.
	15503	„	John Lacs, —	J. D. Cramer Roberts, —	Breckage, ..
	15576	„	Michael Murphy, ...	Philip Richard Cram, Mary Cram of full age, Henry K. Cram, and John Cram, by Henrietta Cram, chief guardian, and Elizabeth L. M. Cram, a person of unsound mind not so found.	Lacaheen, ...
	15560	„	Michael Callaghan, ...	Thomas Clarke, ...	Knockbeg, ..
					Total, ...

COUNTY OF

Assistant Commissioners—					
. L. Doyle (Legal). A. N. Coyne. G. S. Bolster.	1473	Mar. 17,	Sarah Neill, —	Sir John Godfrey, —	Knockbrack and another.

COUNTY OF

Assistant Commissioners—					
L. Doyle (Legal). R. Donovan, Wm. Walpole.	1749	Mar. 22,	Thomas Stokes, ...	Annie Power, ... —	Kildimo, ..

CIVIL BILL

PROVINCE OF

COUNTY OF

FIRST STATUTORY TERM.

CORK—*continued*.

Extent of Holdings Acres &c.	Poor Law Valuation.	Former Rent.	Judicial Rent.	Observations.	Value of Tenancy.
A. R. P.	£ s. d.	£ s. d.	£ s. d.		£ s. d.
66 1 13	26 5 0	29 10 0	20 10 0		
141 1 03	70 10 0	59 6 10	56 10 0		
153 3 29	81 10 0	86 0 0	63 10 0		
61 0 0	70 5 0	23 12 0	16 0 0		
190 1 12	270 0 0	204 1 10	275 16 6		

KERRY.

61 2 13	31 13 0	58 0 0	33 0 0		

TIPPERARY.

30 3 34	31 0 0	37 0 0	30 6 0		

COURTS.

ULSTER.

ARMAGH.

Extent of Holdings Acres &c.	Poor Law Valuation.	Former Rent.	Judicial Rent.	Observations.	Value of Tenancy.
A. R. P.	£ s. d.	£ s. d.	£ s. d.		£ s. d.
2 2 0	5 0 0	3 6 6	2 7 6	By consent.	
4 0 0	7 10 0	5 10 6	4 0 0	do.	
6 2 0	12 10 0	8 16 0	6 7 6		

E

County Court Judge	Record Number	Date of Order	Name of Tenant	Name of Landlord	Townland
		1897.			
D. FITZGERALD, Q.C.	145	Jan. 11,	Michael Byrne,	Whitelaw, Messrs,	Glenn East,

County Court Judge	Record Number	Date of Order	Name of Tenant	Name of Landlord	Townland
W. H. KELLY, Q.C.	223	Feb. 6,	Patrick J. Murphy, ...	Sir Augustus V. Foster, Bt.,	Haggardstown, ...
	224	,,	Arthur Hanratty, ...	Capel & Manraly, ...	Ballymascanlan,
	225	,,	John Rogan, ...	Pakenham Drury, ...	Monasterin,
	229	,,	Michael Callan, ...	Earl Roswell, ...	Carrickrobin,
	228	,,	Thomas Magill, ...	do. ...	Carrickabane etc.
	237	,,	Sarah M'Donald, ...	C. E. Dobbin, ...	North Marsh,
	230	,,	Philip J. Daly, Rep. of Mary Daly, decd.	do. ...	do.
	236	,,	Edward M'Keon, ...	do. ...	do.
	235	,,	John Murphy, ...	do. ...	do.
	234	,,	do. ...	do. ...	do.
	233	,,	Peter Callan, ...	do. ...	do.
	231	,,	Edward M'Keon, ...	do. ...	do.
	231	,,	Peter O'Hagan, ...	do. ...	do.
	238	Feb. 7,	Michael Murphy, ...	Lord Carlingford, ...	Haggardstown,
					Total,

County Court Judge	Record Number	Date of Order	Name of Tenant	Name of Landlord	Townland
J. A. CURRAN, Q.C.	917	Jan. 20,	Lawrence Burnett,	John Wright and others,	Aughamore,
	909	,,	Patrick Malley,	do. ...	Clooncara,
					Total,

LEINSTER.

KILKENNY.

Area of Holding acres.	Poor Law Valuation.	Former Rent.	Judicial Rent.	Observations.	Value of Tenancy.
A. R. P.	£ s. d.	£ s. d.	£ s. d.		£ s. d.
44 0 0	17 0 0	16 0 0	16 0 0		

LOUTH.

28 0 06	31 10 0	23 9 2	40 16 0		
4 3 26	4 16 0	6 0 0	4 0 0		
34 2 38	7 5 0	10 0 0	7 0 0		
20 0 0	13 6 0	14 0 0	11 5 0		
44 0 0	22 0 0	34 6 0	20 0 0		
4 3 63	7 10 0	13 3 0	9 11 0		
4 0 53	7 5 0	9 18 0	4 11 6		
4 0 8	10 0 0	13 3 0	16 12 6		
3 0 25	11 6 0	17 0 0	13 13 8		
11 0 20	13 16 0	23 1 0	17 15 0		
11 1 36	18 10 0	22 18 6	16 10 0		
23 0 11	27 6 0	36 14 0	29 1 3		
4 3 1	6 10 0	6 6 0	6 10 8		
4 0 30	6 10 0	7 10 0	5 10 0		
151 0 38	186 6 6	244 5 8	172 18 0		

WESTMEATH.

CIVIL BILL COURTS.

FIRST STATUTORY TERM

PROVINCE OF

COUNTY OF

County Court Judge.	Record Number	Date of Order	Name of Tenant.	Name of Landlord.	Townland.
		1897.			
G. Waters, &c.	3355	Jan. 7,	Hugh Slevin, ...	Charles G. Tottenham and anor., Trustees of Sarah A. Tottenham.	Killyclogher, —
	3397	"	Michael O'Brien, —	Sarah Ashwood and anor.	Downahinny, —
	3375	"	Nixon Hetherington,	do. —	Knockavelim, —
	3394	"	Catherine Patterson,	do. ...	Derrievanny Up.
	3393	"	Patrick M'Fadden, ...	do. ...	Derrievanny Lr. and another.
	3396	"	Myles Tallon, —	do. ...	Derrievanby Up.
	3375	"	John Honeyman, Admr. of Henry Honeyman, decd.	Major M. N. G. Kane, ...	Dunimbrohid —
	3393	"	Eliza J. Armstrong...	Archibald Cullen, ...	Carve, —
	3393	"	Richard Tate, ...	Patrick Gaffney, ...	Clanbolannale, —
					Total, —

PROVINCE OF

COUNTY OF

		1897.			
W. S. Bane, &c.	3594	Jan. 14,	Michael Kelleher, —	Col. H. V. Stuart, —	Annsbole, —
	3796	"	Daniel Hyde, ...	John Bembill, —	... Scraheenmore —
J. G. Newman, &c.	3177	Feb. 2.	John Shanahan, ...	Peter Twan Godsell, —	Monagirara, —
	3178	" 1898	John Roche, —	Miss Kate Pigott, ...	Castlelerry, —
	3150	Nov. 7, 1897.	Lawrence Going, ...	Earl of Listowell, ...	Gurvonba, —
	3178	Jan. 16.	Bartho. M'Auliffe, ...	Henry O Bayley, ...	Dromin, —

CONNAUGHT.

LEITRIM.

Area of Holdings. Roods.	Poor Law Valuation.	Former Rent.	Judicial Rent.	Observations.	Value of Tenancy.
A. R. P.	£ s. d.	£ s. d.	£ s. d.		£ s. d.
10 3 30	2 10 0	3 3 0	3 0 0		
17 8 15	7 0 0	5 0 0	4 17 0		
14 1 15	9 0 0	5 10 0	4 18 0		
15 3 11	7 5 0	11 17 4	6 10 0		
19 0 0	14 15 0	11 0 0	6 7 6		
15 0 15	9 15 0	9 1 0	5 15 0		
65 0 10	11 15 0	12 9 6	8 0 0		
75 0 10	19 0 0	21 4 6	18 3 0		
4 0 0	unascertained.	1 13 0	1 7 0		
103 0 6	76 0 0	64 6 6	50 16 6		

MUNSTER.

CORK.

7 0 14	3 5 0	6 4 8	2 5 0		
49 1 15	9 10 0	11 3 6	7 10 0		
13 8 0	17 10 0	21 6 9	13 0 0		
41 5 5	57 5 0	61 7 0	55 0 6		
9 8 0	4 5 0	6 10 0	3 5 0		
15 0 0	34 0 0	61 7 8	33 16 0		
145 2 17	157 15 0	163 15 8	113 13 0		

LAND LAW (IRELAND) ACT, 1887.

LEASEHOLDERS.

FIRST STATUTORY TERM.

IRISH LAND COMMISSION.

FIRST STATUTORY TERM.

PROVINCE OF

COUNTY OF

Name of Assistant Commissioners by whom Cases were decided.	Record Number.	Date of Order.	Name of Tenant.	Name of Landlord.	Townland.
Assistant Commissioners— W. F. Bailey (Legal). Jas. MacKenzie. A. Bentall.	11561	1877. March 12,	William Gamble, —	Duke of Bexcleuch and another, Trustees of Duke of Manchester.	Armagh.

COUNTY OF

| Assistant Commissioners— J. H. Ross (Legal). F. O'Callaghan. L. Oakley. | 7485 | March 17, | Thomas Rally, | ... | William Phillips and another, Trustees of C. R. Lloyd, deceased. | Drumgilf &c. |

COUNTY OF

| Assistant Commissioners— C. H. Tearing (Legal). M. H. Franols. J. A. Smith. | 12375 13512 | January 8, March 22, | John Peopler, James M'Coogan, | ... ... | Alexander Black, Marquis Conyngham, | — — | K Clynon, Navney, Total. | — — — |

COUNTY OF

| Assistant Commissioners— W. F. Bailey (Legal). C. W. Thornton. B. O'C. Dovalas. | 12012 12013 | March 5, " | Alexander Hill, Hugh Steward & assr., | — | Col. Alexander Gracey, Henry Maguire, | — ... | Ballyboa&, Carlguat&, Total. | — — — |

COUNTY OF

| Assistant Commissioners— C. H. Tearing (Legal). H. Johnston. M. M'Elligott. | 8137 | Jan. 31, | Francis Ramsey, | ... | Thomas Crowe, | ... | O'neal. | — |

ULSTER.

ARMAGH.

Extent of Holding, Acres.	Poor Law Valuation.	Terms Rent.	Judicial Rent.	Observations.	Value of Tenancy.
A. R. P.	£ s. d.	£ s. d.	£ s. d.		£ s. d.
18 3 31	—	19 11 10	18 11 10		

CAVAN.

15 8 15	10 10 0	9 10 1	8 0 0		

DONEGAL.

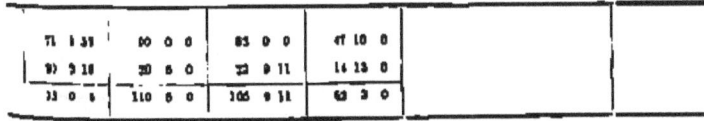

33 7 36	18 10 0	16 16 0	19 16 0	By estimate.	
73 0 0	49 15 0	64 12 0	11 12 3		
108 3 36	43 5 0	40 3 0	64 14 3		

DOWN.

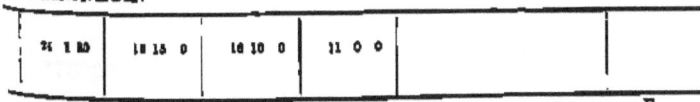

71 1 39	90 0 0	83 0 0	47 10 0		
9) 9 19	20 6 0	22 9 11	14 13 0		
33 0 9	110 6 0	105 9 11	62 3 0		

FERMANAGH.

24 1 80	18 15 0	16 10 0	11 0 0		

F

FIRST STATUTORY TERM.

COUNTY OF

Names of Assistant Commissioners by whom Cases were decided.	Record Number	Date of Order.	Name of Tenant.	Name of Landlord.	Townland.
Assistant Commissioners— D. Tuckey (Legal), R. Spendle. J. M. Kelly.	5401	1887. March 8,	James Buchanan, —	Rev. Robert Kyle, —	Craigtown, —

PROVINCE OF

COUNTY OF

Assistant Commissioners— L. Doyle (Legal), A. N. Conyn. G. S. Bolster.	1676	Feb. 3,	Matthew Reid, —	Lt.-Col. W. J. Alexander.	Garristown and another.
	1675	„	' Do. —	do. —	do.
	1675	March 20,	Matthew Kennedy, —	Rev. H. C. Burroughs and another	Tymon North —
	1641	„	Nathaniel Hann, —	W. De C. Ireland, —	Baldonstown, —
					Total, ..

QUEEN'S

Assistant Commissioners— M. T. Chase (Legal). F. M. Carroll. J. Hawkins.	1861	March 17,	Thomas Kehoe, —	Rev. R. Fitzgerald, —	Craigmahorn, —

COUNTY OF

Assistant Commissioners— M. T. Chase (Legal). T. A. Dillow. J. A. O'Kelly.	7404	March 10,	Francis J. McDonald,	Miss Susanna R. Davis and others.	Clarinbad, —

FIRST STATUTORY TERM.

LONDONDERRY.

Extent of Holding. Statute.	Poor Law Valuation.	Former Rent.	Judicial Rent.	Observations.	Value of Tenancy.
A. R. P.	£ s. d.	£ s. d.	£ s. d.		£ s. d.
43 1 10	24 0 0	34 7 0	34 14 0		

LEINSTER.

DUBLIN.

31 1 37	unascertained,	38 8 0	43 8 0	By consent.	
43 0 30	do.	31 10 0	19 13 0	do.	
38 1 25	198 0 0	260 0 0	140 0 0		
103 0 12	103 0 0	204 1 0	185 0 0		
144 1 24	301 0 0	533 0 0	347 18 0		

COUNTY.

143 1 37	unascertained,	113 4 11	64 8 0		

WICKLOW.

CIVIL BILL COURTS.

FIRST STATUTORY TERM.

PROVINCE OF

COUNTY OF

Names of Assistant Commissioners by whom Cases were decided.	Record No.	Date of Order.	Name of Tenant.	Name of Landlord.	Townland.
Assistant Commissioners—		1877.			
L. Doyle (Legal).	9707	Mar. 16,	John Gaffney, —	Col. Henry H. Archer, ...	Moymore, —
O. O'Keeffe.	6424	„ 9,	Pats O'Neill, —	C. R. A. MacDermott, ...	Limerick —
J. Ross.					Total, —

COUNTY OF

Assistant Commissioners—		1877.			
L. Doyle (Legal).	18129	Mar. 1,	Thomas Murphy, continued by Catherine Murphy,	John Laffan, continued by X. M. C. Laffan, a minor, by A. M. C. Laffan,	Sergeants Orchard or Farrenfarris
E. G. Pratt.	15567	„ 23,	Ress, Daly, ...	H. M. Dennehie and ors.,	Cahergal, ...
R. Moriarty.	13566	„	Daniel O'Mahony, —	Miss O. H. Cummins, —	Ballyvodane, —
L. Doyle (Legal).	13519	Mar. 13,	John Cashman, ...	Davy June Smith, ...	Crosbyview, —
S. G. Pratt.	13450	„	Michael Cashman, ...	do. ...	do. —
					Total, —

CIVIL BILL

PROVINCE OF

COUNTY OF

County Court Judge.	Record Number.	Date of Order.	Name of Tenant.	Name of Landlord.	Townland.
County Court Judge—		1877.			
W. S. Ross, Q.C.	1893	Jan. 73,	Catherine A. Fuller,	Earl of Fenton, —	Ballytunmore ...
	3907	„ 14,	John Geogan,	William H. H. Massy, ...	Maningsharts —
					Total, ...

MUNSTER.

CLARE

Area of Holding Statute	Poor Law Valuation.	Former Rent.	Judicial Rent.	Observations.	Value of Tenancy.
A. R. P.	£ s. d.	£ s. d.	£ s. d.		£ s. d.
173 2 30	69 10 0	70 5 0	56 5 0		
16? 2 5	54 0 0	110 0 0	50 0 0		
637 0 64	123 10 0	180 5 0	105 5 0		

CORK.

2 0 25	5 15 0	20 0 0	8 0 0		
11 1 27	16 0 0	30 0 0	10 5 0		
8 1 16	unsurveyed.	11 13 6	10 5 0		
74 2 10	60 15 0	54 2 4	49 8 0	Form 36.	
71 1 8	61 10 0	51 2 4	49 5 0	Do.	
167 2 8	54 0 0	169 17 4	132 0 0		

COURTS.

MUNSTER.

CORK.

MONTH OF MARCH, 1897.

SECOND STATUTORY TERM.

SECOND STATUTORY TERM

PROVINCE OF

COUNTY OF

Names of Assistant Commissioners by whom Case was decided	Record Number	Date of Order	Name of Tenant	Name of Landlord	Townland
Assistant Commissioners—		1897.			
D. Tighe (Legal), L. W. Byrne, G. Fitzgerald.	1672	Feb. 25,	John Steele,	James Henry,	Ballyclough Pa.
W. F. Bailey (Legal), W. H. O. Byrne, J. Armstrong.	226	March 26,	W. J. Palmer,	H. H. Stewart,	Killealy.
	128	„	Mrs. Ellen Stevenson,	S. Birch and ors., Trus. of the Ulster Permanent Building Society,	Ballyrashane,
	140	„	Malcolm Crawford,	do.	do.
	141	„	Andrew Montgomery,	do.	do.
	138	„	Thomas Mawhinney,	do.	do.
	633	„	Jane M'Knight,	do.	do.
T. Davidson, S. Wilson.	118	March 6,	Jane Fisher,	James Carlisle,	Fernisky.
	99	„	Samuel Adams,	John Young and another, Trus. of K. H. Jones, deceased.	Gortreagh,
	90	„	William G. Adams,	do.	do.
	69	„	Arthur Murphy,	Samuel Thompson,	Taylorstown,
	181	„	Thomas Birt,	Frederick D. Crommelin,	Shanny East,
	180	„	Denis Birt,	do.	do.
	171	„	Gilbert Fishell,	Dr. W. Smyth and anty., Reps. of Thomas Harris,	Taylorstown,
	179	„	Thomas M'Keown,	Richard Dynes,	Tunkleagh.
	178	„	Robert Madden and another.	do.	do.
	197	„	Ellen M'Keown,	do.	do.
	187	„	Adam Bell, junior,	do.	Gortfield,
	376	„	William Miller,	do.	do.
	175	„	Joseph Crawford,	do.	do.
	156	„	John M'Caughey,	do.	Killyougan,
	153	„	Catherine Boyd,	do.	do.

ULSTER.

ANTRIM.

Rent of Holding. Acres.	Poor Law Valuation.	Rent of Holding prior to Creation of First Statutory Term.	Judicial Rent for First Statutory Term.	Judicial Rent for Second Statutory Term.	Observations.	Value of Tenancy.
A. R. P.	£ s. d.	£ s. d.	£ s. d.	£ s. d.		£ s. d.
16 0 1	18 0 0	16 17 4	14 6 6	30 8 0		
47 0 5	51 14 0	49 18 4	41 16 0	50 5 0		
57 1 25	18 2 0	29 8 0	22 0 0	14 14 0		
17 6 0	9 5 6	—	12 15 0	9 5 0	Holding changed since 1881.	
13 1 20	4 19 0	11 1 6	8 0 0	8 0 0		
57 2 26	13 5 0	25 0 0	18 5 0	11 10 0		
18 0 55	10 0 0	12 12 0	10 0 0	7 2 0		
7 0 20	5 7 0	8 0 0	6 12 0	5 5 0		
16 2 20	13 10 0	18 6 0	11 5 0	8 0 0		
15 1 12	19 15 0	20 5 5	18 0 0	7 10 0		
66 2 0	80 0 0	22 18 1	25 5 0	20 0 0		
13 1 0	8 10 0	9 17 0	8 10 0	4 17 0		
14 0 0	12 0 0	17 17 6	11 15 0	8 15 0		
20 0 0	18 10 0	20 4 6	21 0 0	16 5 0		
23 1 14	19 5 0	21 0 0	15 17 0	12 8 0		
71 3 20	14 0 0	16 0 0	11 10 0	6 0 0		
28 1 5	13 10 0	14 0 0	11 5 0	9 8 0		
15 1 0	13 15 0	17 0 0	11 10 0	10 10 0		
20 0 15	21 10 0	29 0 0	20 5 0	12 10 0		
14 0 20	21 10 0	17 0 0	15 14 0	8 15 0		
20 0 0	17 15 0	22 0 0	16 5 0	9 10 0		
15 2 19	19 5 0	14 0 0	11 10 0	8 10 0		

G

SECOND STATUTORY TERM.

COUNTY OF

Name of Assistant Commissioners by whom Cases were decided.	Record Number.	Date of Order.	Name of Tenant.	Name of Landlord.	Townland.
Assistant Commissioners—		1887.			
T. DAVIDSON, & WILSON.	184	March 5,	Wilson M'Keown, ...	Richard Dyott,	... Killyvougan,
	183	„	James Roe,	do.	do.
	212	„	David Gibson,	do.	do.
	181	„	Samuel Adams,	do.	do.
	174	„	W. J. Barkley,	do.	do.
	173	„	Isabella M'Donnell, ...	do.	Aughnacloy,
	189	„	Robert Lowry,	do.	Gortaham,
	186	„	William Wallace,	do.	do.
	173	„	John Barkley,	do.	do.
	184	„	Mathew M'Caughey,	do.	do.
	180	„	James M'Keown, ...	do.	Tullynahinion,
J. MACBETH, L. W. BYRNE.	23	March 1,	Samuel J. Dunlop,	Provincial Bank of Ireland,	Clogher, & co.,
	27	„	Do. ...	do.	do.
	37	„	James Lyons,	James A. Henney,	Coraghen,
	36	„	Daniel Patterson,	do.	do.
	35	„	Robert Patterson, ...	do.	Ballyobn,
	32	„	Robert Ambrose, ...	do.	Ballyclough,
	5	„	Samuel Steele,	do.	do.
D. TRENT (Legal), T. DAVIDSON, C. H. BRABTER.	175	March 10,	John M'Cann,	John F. W. Hodges,	Dungannel,
	277	„	Grace Campbell,	do.	Craigbalad,
	196	„	Wm. Ross,	do.	do.
	193	„	Charles O'Neill,	do.	do.
	294	„	William Quilly,	do.	Cargans,
	293	„	John M'Killop,	do.	Craigbalad,
	547	„	Mary Scully,	F. A. D. Crommelin,	Cherry Roe,
	548	„	John Donaghy,	do.	do.
	345	„	Patrick Burns,	do.	do.
	544	„	John Delargy,	do.	do.
	543	„	John M'Cambridge, ...	do.	do.
	542	„	Hannah O'Neill, ...	do.	do.

4	5	0	10	0	0	8	10	0	4	17
11	10	0	15	0	0	11	15	0	8	5
20	0	0	10	0	0	32	0	0	11	10
27	15	0	28	0	0	20	0	0	11	10
9	15	0	11	0	0	8	0	0	4	0
14	0	0	19	0	0	14	0	0	8	0
28	0	0	68	10	3	45	0	0	26	2
25	10	0	108	15	4	130	0	0	53	14
17	0	0	55	7	6	65	10	0	27	9
35	5	0	42	0	0	54	10	0	29	18
17	15	0	25	5	5	16	5	0	16	15
57	5	0	39	5	11	57	0	0	23	9
23	10	0	44	15	5	38	10	0	27	5
18	5	0	17	5	5	18	7	0	10	0
4	5	0	15	0	0	8	15	0	4	13
7	0	0	18	13	5	8	5	0	5	15
7	15	0	19	0	0	9	15	0	5	15

IRISH LAND COMMISSION.

SECOND STATUTORY TERM.

COUNTY OF

Name of Assistant Commissioners by whom Cases were decided.	Record Number.	Date of Order.	Name of Tenant.	Name of Landlord.			Townland.	
Assistant Commissioners—		1897.						
D. Twigg (Legal). T. Davison. C. H. Roberts.	341	March 18,	John Reid,	...	F. A. D. Crommelin,	...	Shirly, Esq.	..
	311	"	Samuel M'Clement,	...	do.	—	—	do.	
	810	"	Thomas Sterling,	...	do.	...	—	do.	
	309	"	Patrick Carey,	...	do.	...	—	do.	
	308	"	Do.,	...	do.	—	...	do.	
	332	"	John M'Cormack,	—	do.	...	...	do.	
	391	"	William Owens,	—	do.	—	—	do.	
	268	"	Arthur M'Allister,	...	do.	...	—	do.	
	346	"	John M'Cann,	—	do.	—	—	do.	
	363	"	Patrick Burke,	—	do.	...	...	do.	
	354	"	Michael Doherty,	—	do.	—	—	do.	
	361	"	John Rea,	—	do.	—	...	do.	
	360	"	Archibald Haughian,	—	do.	—	—	do.	
	369	"	Do.,	—	do.	—	—	do.	
	348	"	James Kennedy,	—	do.	—	—	do.	
	817	"	Patrick Carey,	...	do.	—	—	do.	
	316	"	Thomas Durnan,	—	do.	—	—	do.	
	316	"	James Boyd,	—	do.	—	—	do.	
	314	"	Robert Steele,	...	do.	—	—	do.	
	313	"	Margaret Carey,	—	do.	...	—	do.	
	312	"	Isabella Price,	—	do.	—	—	do.	
	323	"	John Carey,	—	do.	—	—	do.	
	431	"	James Murdoch,	—	do.	—	—	do.	
	330	"	Hugh Burns,	—	do.	—	—	do.	
	328	"	Archibald M'Quillan,	—	do.	—	—	do.	
	327	"	Harrison, Durnan,	—	do.	...	—	do.	
	324	"	John Maxwell,	—	do.	...	—	do.	
	326	"	Houston Palmer,	—	do.	...	—	do.	
	322	"	John M'Cartney,	...	do.	—	—	do.	
	321	"	John Kelly,	...	do.	—	—	do.	
	320	"	Robert Kelly,	—	do.	...	...	do.	
							Total	—

SECOND STATUTORY TERM.

ANTRIM—*continued.*

Area of Holding Acres	Poor Law Valuation	Rent of Holding prior to Standard of First Statutory Term	Judicial Rent for First Statutory Term	Judicial Rent for Second Statutory Term	Observations	Value of Tenancy
A. R. P.	£ s. d.	£ s. d.	£ s. d.	£ s. d.		£ s. d.
14 3 0	5 10 0	6 6 0	6 0 0	5 5 0		
20 0 0	6 18 0	13 0 0	8 9 0	5 13 0		
20 1 37	3 5 0	7 1 0	4 0 0	3 10 0		
20 3 20	6 10 0	9 0 0	6 15 0	4 10 0		
11 1 10	4 10 0	7 18 0	5 6 0	3 4 0		
11 2 10	5 10 0	7 6 0	6 0 0	3 12 0		
12 0 0	8 5 0	18 18 0	11 5 0	6 0 0		
17 2 30	5 0 0	3 17 0	5 6 0	8 17 0		
18 0 19	5 10 0	9 13 0	6 0 0	5 0 0		
5 2 0	3 10 0	6 11 0	4 10 0	3 0 0		
11 0 20	6 0 0	6 5 0	5 10 0	5 5 0		
19 2 0	7 0 0	13 0 0	8 5 0	4 15 0		
13 0 0	8 10 0	8 10 0	6 15 0	6 10 0		
16 1 13	5 15 0	7 0 0	4 18 0	5 0 0		
60 3 30	3 18 0	6 0 0	5 5 0	5 6 0		
13 2 20	3 0 0	4 10 0	3 6 0	5 3 0		
16 2 10	8 16 0	10 0 0	7 5 0	5 6 0		
11 1 10	5 5 0	6 0 0	4 5 0	3 10 0		
10 1 0	6 0 0	8 5 0	6 13 0	6 15 0		
13 0 0	6 5 0	7 13 0	5 3 0	5 7 0		
6 0 0	3 16 0	6 16 0	5 0 0	3 6 0		
4 1 36	6 6 0	1 13 0	5 16 0	5 30 0		
1 0 0	3 15 0	7 0 0	4 13 0	6 6 0		
14 6 0	6 10 0	10 6 0	6 15 0	5 17 0		
9 2 19	6 0 0	5 11 0	6 16 0	3 18 0		
7 2 6	6 6 0	5 10 0	3 17 0	3 6 0		
17 6 0	6 0 0	3 16 0	5 16 0	3 12 0		
22 0 0	1 16 0	6 0 0	6 0 0	6 17 0		
14 5 0	4 5 0	8 10 0	4 0 0	5 17 0		
4 2 6	3 5 0	5 0 0	3 10 0	3 10 0		
18 3 30	7 10 0	18 5 0	9 10 0	6 16 0		
1,497 1 16	4,103 19 0	1,520 15 10	1,164 16 0	779 9 8		

SECOND STATUTORY TERM.

COUNTY OF

Name of Assistant Commissioners by Whom Cases were heard.	Record Number	Date of Cases	Name of Tenant.	Name of Landlord.	Townland.
Assistant Commissioners—		1887.			
W. F. Bailey (Legal). J. MacKerrell. A. Birrall.	1025	March 19.	John Johnson,	Duke of Bamford and anr., Trustees of the Duke of Manchester.	Glasserto,
	1445	Jan. 19.	William Robinson,	Henrietta Morwood and another.	Carbrackey,
	1597	"	Anne and Sarah Kernan,	Lord Lurgan,	Umhem,
	1490	"	Thomas Porter,	Henrietta Morwood and another.	Carbrackey,
	1494	"	William Jones,	do.	Carbrackagh,
	1445	"	Richard Weatheral and another.	Mrs. A. O. Craig,	Poyleg,
	1003	"	David Abraham,	Mrs. Galbraeton Carleton,	K Sturgin,
	1004	"	Thomas Lyons,	The Duke of Bamford and another, Trustees of the Duke of Manchester.	Clanrole,
	1035	"	Samuel Bullick,	do.	Drumaguan,
	1053	"	John Midkiff,	do.	Tarms,
	1118	"	Mordecai Johnson,	do.	Kavahnane and another.
	1515	"	Thomas Gilbert,	do.	Ballimeart,
	1471	"	Robert Prim,	do.	do.
	1472	"	William J. Church,	do.	Armagh,
	1039	"	William Metcalfe,	Heather A. Barnes Van Straubie.	Lower Sebo,
	1526	"	James Wright,	R. H. Farrell and another,	Drummintlly,
	1520	"	John M'Cann,	Rev. Geo. Yeates and anr.	Drumgor,
J. H. Enes (Legal). M. J. Paterson. J. S. G. Mowman.	1563	March 2.	James Hughes,	Anne M'Arde,	Mulland,
	1629	"	Hugh Morris,	James Hamerly,	Rathbinland,
	996	"	Henry M'Nabon,	John Johnston,	Pladuke,
	997	"	Patrick Hughes,	Francis J. Johnston and another.	Umaciam,
	916	"	Arthur Hughes,	do.	do.
	1563	"	Mary Gordon, Rep. of Thomas Gordon.	Captain Ralph M'G. D. Shehan.	Alamanakin,
	1533	"	William M'Kelvey,	do.	do.
	1500	"	Mary Milligan,	do.	do.
	1011	"	John Caswell,	do.	do.
	1881	"	Andrew M'Ka,	do.	do.
	1837	"	William Mauk,	William Read,	Tullyvallen,
	1547	"	Charles Emey,	do.	do.
	1576	"	Denis M'Arde,	do.	do.
	1545	"	James Patterson,	do.	do.

SECOND STATUTORY TERM.

ARMAGH.

Extent of Holding. Acres.	Poor Law Valuation.	Rent of Holding prior to existing First Statutory Term.	Judicial Rent for First Statutory Term.	Judicial Rent for Second Statutory Term.	Observations.	Value of Tenancy.
A. R. P.	£ s. d.	£ s. d.	£ s. d.	£ s. d.		£ s. d.
0 1 0	13 0 0	9 13 0	8 10 0	6 0 0		
0 0 10	10 15 0	9 15 0	8 15 0	5 5 0		
42 1 30	51 10 0	58 0 0	43 10 0	30 10 0		
56 0 0	97 10 0	99 0 0	55 0 0	57 10 0		
19 3 0	16 5 0	15 9 6	14 10 0	9 0 0		
54 3 0	52 15 0	59 10 0	45 0 0	39 10 0		
35 3 0	31 0 0	43 0 0	37 10 0	17 0 0		
4 1 15	5 14 0	6 13 0	4 10 0	3 0 0		
13 3 30	18 15 0	17 3 11	11 10 0	10 3 0		
5 0 0	7 0 0	7 15 0	8 10 0	1 5 0		
43 3 30	34 5 0	51 10 8	45 0 0	30 7 6		
13 1 30	20 5 0	27 0 0	14 0 0	9 5 0		
36 0 11	45 0 0	70 15 0	55 0 0	29 5 0		
1 0 20	7 10 0	11 3 7	7 0 0	6 17 0		
63 3 21	62 5 0	54 3 0	25 0 0	20 0 0		
10 1 0	19 15 0	19 13 5	15 0 0	5 3 6		
11 3 20	17 0 0	17 15 7	14 0 0	5 14 0		
23 0 20	15 10 0	18 15 10	11 5 0	8 16 3		
14 3 30	12 15 5	17 15 6	10 0 0	12 7 8		
13 3 14	10 5 0	11 5 5	6 10 0	5 5 0		
6 0 0	5 5 0	5 3 5	3 13 5	3 15 6		
6 0 30	3 15 0	5 0 0	3 3 0	3 3 0		
17 0 30	19 15 0	19 15 3	16 0 0	13 3 4		
50 3 30	13 0 0	13 14 6	13 10 0	5 5 3		
25 3 30	63 0 0	54 3 11	10 0 0	16 10 9		
45 3 25	17 0 0	18 3 3	13 15 0	10 13 9		
6 0 0	5 5 0	6 11 9	8 15 0	3 1 3		
51 1 3	15 15 0	17 4 9	13 10 0	8 15 9		
30 0 30	20 15 0	23 13 0	15 0 0	17 10 8		
13 1 10	9 3 0	11 11 10	7 15 0	6 17 1		
47 0 0	34 10 0	61 13 5	34 0 0	34 4 4		

IRISH LAND COMMISSION.

SECOND STATUTORY TERM.

COUNTY OF

Names of Assistant Commissioners by whom Cases were decided.	Record Number.	Date of Order.	Name of Tenant.	Name of Landlord.	Townland.
Assistant Commissioners— J. H. Knox (Legal). M. S. Pattumann. J. S. S. Moubray.	1344	1897 March 9,	Bridget Murphy, —	William Reed,	Tullyvallen
	1343	„	John Henry, —	do — —	do
	1241	„	Thomas M'Murray, —	do — —	do
	1240	„	Rose Murphy, Ltd. Admin. of Thomas Murphy.	do — —	do
	1239	„	James Grealer, —	do — —	do
	1236	„	James M'Creesh, —	do — —	do
	1228	„	John Nugent, —	do — —	do
	944	„	Stephen Meehan, —	Robert J. M'Geough,	Dorsey, Tullynah
	943	„	John Waters, —	do — —	do
	949	„	Do., —	do — —	Dorsey, Cavan
	911	„	Owen Small, —	do — —	Aughnakeil
	923	„	Catharine Murphy, —	do — —	do
	941	„	Ann Mulholland, —	do — —	do
	944	„	Bernard Loye, —	do — —	Dorsey, Shean
	943	„	John Loye (Michael),	do — —	Umman,
	942	„	Henry Loye (Pat), —	do — —	do
	941	„	Francis Loye (junior),	do — —	do
	908	„	John M'Creesh, —	do — —	Castial,
	940	„	Francis Loy (George),	do — —	do
	1132	„	Pat Garvey, Rep. of John Garvey,	do — —	Ummericrove
	949	„	James Meehan, —	do — —	do
	934	„	Catharine Crilly, —	do — —	do
	948	„	Bridget Quigley, —	do — —	Dorsey, Shean
	960	„	Bridget Short, —	do — —	do
	1128	„	Robert Coulter, —	do — —	do
	1118	„	Patrick M'Coy, —	do — —	Dorsey,
	938	„	Edward Quigley, —	do — —	do
	907	„	Do., —	do — —	do
	956	„	Mary M'Creesh, —	do — —	do
	854	„	Michael M'Cann, —	do — —	do
	950	„	Thos. Meehan (Hugh),	do — —	do
	948	„	Thos. Meehan (John),	do — —	do
	957	„	Rose Meehan, —	do — —	do
	946	„	Mary Meehan, —	do — —	do

SECOND STATUTORY TERM

ARMAGH—continued.

Extent of Holding Statute Measure	Poor Law Valuation	Rent of Holding prior to creation of First Statutory Term	Judicial Rent for First Statutory Term	Judicial Rent for Second Statutory Term	Observations	Value of Timber
A. R. P.	£ s. d.	£ s. d.	£ s. d.	£ s. d.		£ s. d.
17 1 35	16 18 0	18 7 6	9 5 0	5 16 7		
26 0 19	30 0 0	32 15 2	25 10 0	18 6 6		
10 0 30	7 16 0	8 9 8	8 10 0	4 19 4		
11 2 0	7 10 0	8 4 2	7 0 0	5 13 5		
5 1 25	3 15 0	6 1 1	4 0 0	6 0 1		
6 1 10	5 15 0	7 10 0	5 6 0	5 9 2		
11 2 30	12 0 0	13 13 10	9 15 0	7 1 11		
11 0 34	7 0 0	8 10 1	7 0 0	4 19 10		
5 1 4	8 15 0	7 11 8	1 13 6	1 6 3		
8 0 16	1 15 0	8 7 0	1 10 0	1 1 4		
14 1 6	7 6 0	11 7 5	7 0 0	6 6 3		
38 3 20	16 0 0	18 10 3	9 5 0	7 0 1		
5 2 3	1 15 0	8 5 5	1 10 0	1 0 0		
7 3 10	8 10 0	6 4 6	4 10 0	3 7 1		
23 3 17	8 10 0	11 0 6	4 17 6	5 18 6		
13 1 10	6 6 0	7 8 1	6 6 0	3 10 0		
9 5 25	5 10 8	6 1 1	4 0 6	4 8 6		
10 2 6	6 18 0	7 14 0	4 13 6	4 4 10		
13 0 0	9 16 0	8 13 0	7 17 6	6 10 10		
13 0 0	6 12 0	7 17 6	3 0 0	3 16 3		
17 5 0	8 6 0	6 13 2	4 10 0	3 0 11		
15 3 9	8 10 0	9 1 8	6 7 6	4 6 3		
15 1 4	6 0 0	6 13 1	4 10 0	4 17 6		
16 3 10	9 6 0	9 16 6	7 16 0	5 19 2		
11 0 37	7 0 0	7 16 0	7 16 0	4 16 0		
22 1 6	12 10 6	11 9 11	10 15 6	8 14 10		
6 5 24	4 10 0	5 12 6	4 7 6	3 6 6		
11 1 16	8 5 0	6 14 11	6 10 0	5 0 6		
37 0 16	18 0 0	20 9 5	16 6 0	11 16 10		
16 1 15	9 6 0	10 3 3	7 0 0	5 0 0		
7 1 10	4 10 0	4 16 0	4 5 0	3 3 6		
9 3 5	5 6 0	5 15 2	4 17 6	5 2 6		
7 3 5	6 10 0	6 6 11	4 10 0	3 4 0		
8 2 30	5 6 0	6 10 5	4 16 0	5 18 6		

SECOND STATUTORY TERM.

COUNTY OF

Name of Assistant Commissioners by whom Case was decided.	Record Number.	Date of Order.	Name of Tenant.	Name of Landlord.	Townland.
Assistant Commissioners—		1887.			
J. H. Eman (Legal), M. S. Patterson, J. H. H. Mottram.	345	Mar. 8,	Felix Mackin, ...	Robert J. M'Clenagh, ...	Dunry, ...
	339	„	Patrick Loughran, ...	do.	do. ...
	338	„	Margaret Johnston, ...	do.	do. ...
	337	„	Michael Hatey, ...	do.	do. ...
	336	„	Ellen Garvey, ...	do.	do. ...
	335	„	Owen Cairy, ...	do.	do. ...
	333	„	John Caffrey, ...	do.	do. ...
	332	„	Denis Bennett, ...	do.	do. ...
	1084	„	Patrick Carnaher and another.	Alexander F. Twemlle and ... sued by Harvey H. Thorpe.	Shancin, ...
					Toal, ...

COUNTY OF

Assistant Commissioners—	21	Feb. 24,	Owen Coyle, ...	James Bartley, ...	Tonagh, ...
M. F. Cahan (Legal), J. D. Boyd, L. Cannay.	66	„	Rose Brady, ...	Earl Annesley, ...	Cavilaga, ...
	44	„	James O'Neill, ...	Gerald F. Holmes & others,	Farkin, ...
	43	„	Thomas Donaghue, ...	do.	do. ...
	37	„	Patrick M'Kenn, ...	do.	do. ...
	80	„	William Best, ...	do.	Clondrew, ...
	49	„	John Moran, ...	do.	do. ...
	48	„	Henry Sheridan, ...	do.	do. ...
	67	„	Thomas Best, ...	do.	do. ...
	54	„	Thomas Wells, ...	F. O. Rowe, ...	E. Kevilly, ...
	53	„	Allen Murphy, ...	do.	do. ...
	54	L.	Charles Robinson, ...	John Garrett Tinlow, ...	Lapland, ...
	63	„	Patrick Malloy, ...	do.	do. ...
J. H. Eman (Legal), F. O'Gallaghar, L. Cannay.	237	Feb. 3,	David Caffrey, ...	Major Henry B. Maxwell,	Drumbo, ...
	116	Mar. 17,	Andrew Brady, ...	Earl Annesley, ...	Cloneavy, ...
	183	„	William Kells, ...	Mrs. Catherine M. Jones,	Tully, ...
	184	„	Thomas Neill, Ltd. Administ. of Edw. Reilly	Mrs. Elizabeth A. Sweeny,	K. Bryhane, ...
	273	„	Alexander M'Donald,	R. F. Ingham and another,	Killaghan, ...

SECOND STATUTORY TERM.

ARMAGH—continued.

Extent of Holding (Statute)	Poor Law Valuation.	Rent of Holding prior to Fixing of First Statutory Term.	Judicial Rent for First Statutory Term.	Judicial Rent for Second Statutory Term.	Observations.	Value of Tenancy.
A. R. P.	£ s. d.	£ s. d.	£ s. d.	£ s. d.		£ s. d.
10 2 23	9 10 0	6 6 8	5 0 0	3 9 10		
16 0 0	18 0 0	17 4 11	9 0 0	8 16 18		
14 1 0	11 8 0	13 10 3	10 10 0	7 10 0		
3 0 16	2 10 0	3 17 0	3 15 0	3 0 0		
43 3 20	27 10 0	30 18 11	28 0 0	17 19 10		
6 1 14	1 14 0	2 19 3	2 10 0	1 11 1		
11 0 4	8 5 0	7 13 8	8 15 0	5 5 0		
11 3 9	7 10 0	7 11 3	6 10 0	4 19 3		
41 0 5	39 15 0	35 10 0	20 0 0	15 11 3		
1,127 1 9	1,042 18 5	1,323 4 5	823 4 0	850 1 8		

CAVAN.

Extent of Holding (Statute)	Poor Law Valuation.	Rent of Holding prior to Fixing of First Statutory Term.	Judicial Rent for First Statutory Term.	Judicial Rent for Second Statutory Term.	Observations.	Value of Tenancy.
23 3 17	13 10 0	21 11 3	15 10 0	14 8 0		
34 2 0	34 5 0	25 17 8	20 0 0	15 18 6		
40 5 0	9 5 0	11 0 0	8 3 6	5 0 0		
26 0 0	11 15 0	15 0 0	11 9 0	6 17 0		
30 1 80	13 15 0	15 5 0	11 5 4	9 4 0		
33 1 30	20 0 0	20 7 5	22 13 0	13 5 0		
10 1 0	6 17 0	5 11 0	5 0 0	4 5 0		
42 5 19	22 15 0	24 2 6	22 0 0	14 7 0		
14 0 16	Unascertained	18 10 6	13 0 0	7 5 0		
15 1 30	8 4 0	9 0 0	7 10 0	5 5 0		
15 0 25	18 0 0	18 15 5	11 6 6	8 13 6		
14 3 30	11 10 0	14 8 8	11 12 0	8 17 6		
50 3 14	35 5 6	43 17 5	32 7 5	23 0 0		
44 3 0	23 10 0	30 0 5	20 0 0	23 10 0	By agreement.	
23 3 19	11 5 0	17 14 3	15 0 0	9 0 0		
34 3 24	40 0 0	42 5 0	28 0 0	17 0 0		
20 3 20	19 0 0	25 7 5	15 5 0	13 19 0		
18 0 25	8 5 0	15 7 0	11 0 0	7 5 0		

B 2

IRISH LAND COMMISSION.

SECOND STATUTORY TERM.

COUNTY OF

Names of Assistant Commissioners by whom Case was decided.	Record Number.	Date of Order.	Name of Tenant.	Name of Landlord.	Townland.
Assistant Commissioners—		1887.			
J. H. Edge (Legal). F. O'Callaghan. L. Crosby.	272	March 17,	William Patterson, —	R. F. Ingham and another,	Killaglare, —
	271	"	William Reilly, —	do. —	do. —
	263	"	Joseph Comely, —	Edward O'Brien, —	Drumbade, —
	261	"	John Coyle, —	do. —	do. —
	260	"	Francis Boylan, —	do. —	do. —
	67	"	Catherine Morgan, —	John G. Tatlow, —	Legaland, —
	226	"	Robert Lowry, —	do. —	do. —
	185	"	Owen Reilly, —	Mrs. G. M. Whyte Venables,	Drumbeara, —
	225	"	Do., —	do. —	do. —
	192	"	John Reilly, —	do. —	Crumbol, —
	811	"	Ellen Lynch, —	Mathew W. Webb, —	Ballagreen, —
	138	"	John M'Govern, —	Jestatio M. O'Reilly, —	Killyolash, —
	137	"	Peter Reilly, —	do. —	do. —
	378	"	John Smith, —	Mrs. Josephine Kelly,	Drumachipin, —
	41	"	Phil Smith, —	James H. M. Garrett, —	Corglasa, —
	69	"	Do., —	do. —	Polladrea, —
	65	"	Peter Smith, —	do. —	Corglasa, —
	64	"	Do., —	do. —	Polladrea, —
	63	"	James Smith, —	do. —	do. —
	60	"	John Smith, —	do. —	do. —
	39	"	John Gallegher, —	do. —	do. —
	38	"	Bernard M'Kenn, —	do. —	do. —
	62	"	Thomas Smith, —	do. —	Lissana, —
	191	"	Thomas Fitzpatrick, —	Tanlagran Tatlow, —	Drummengh, —
	112	"	Ross Coyle, —	do. —	do. —
	164	"	Peter Lynch, —	do. —	do. —
	161	"	James Jann, —	do. —	do. —
	160	"	Catherine Galligan, —	do. —	do. —
	162	"	Terence Reilly, —	do. —	do. —
	214	"	Bernard M'Gaughrin,	George S. Smith, —	Ardlogh, —
	323	"	William Martin, —	do. —	Carintanin, —
	453	"	Anne Evans, Rep. of Thomas Owens,	do. —	do. —
	303	"	James Jackson, —	do. —	Drumenghban, —
	315	"	Edward Boylan, —	do. —	do. —

SECOND STATUTORY TERM.

CAVAN—continued.

Amount of Holding Statute	Poor Law Valuation	Rent of Holding prior to creation of First Statutory Term	Judicial Rent for First Statutory Term	Judicial Rent for Second Statutory Term	Observations	Value of Tenancy
A. R. P.	£ s. d.	£ s. d.	£ s. d.	£ s. d.		£ s. d.
10 0 37	5 0 0	5 14 7	5 5 0	5 0 0		
10 1 19	5 15 0	9 0 0	5 0 0	5 10 0		
84 1 30	14 10 0	20 0 0	14 0 0	11 15 0		
17 3 29	10 0 0	14 10 0	11 0 0	5 4 0		
10 0 0	14 15 0	17 7 5	15 0 5	11 5 0		
61 0 13	37 15 0	43 1 0	37 5 0	70 10 0		
5 0 30	10 10 0	10 15 5	7 10 8	5 15 0		
11 2 17	5 5 0	10 10 0	8 17 6	8 13 0		
3 3 21	4 3 0	5 3 9	5 0 0	9 15 0		
11 3 13	7 0 0	10 7 6	7 15 5	8 3 0		
17 3 23	10 0 0	13 3 0	10 10 0	5 0 0		
5 0 25	Unascertained	4 15 0	1 15 0	1 3 0		
5 0 13	2 10 0	11 5 9	4 5 0	3 10 0		
9 3 11	4 15 0	5 5 3	5 0 0	4 10 0		
38 3 0	15 5 0	30 0 0	17 10 0	11 15 0		
35 0 30	18 0 0	35 15 0	20 0 0	14 10 6		
21 3 0	11 5 0	14 15 5	12 10 0	9 10 0		
1 3 5	3 0 0	8 8 0	3 0 0	1 10 0		
30 3 0	17 5 0	22 3 0	16 0 5	15 0 0		
16 1 7	10 5 0	11 10 6	10 0 0	7 0 0		
15 2 23	11 10 0	21 13 0	15 0 0	11 5 0		
25 3 2	17 5 0	25 0 0	20 0 0	15 0 0		
21 1 0	15 15 0	19 0 0	14 10 0	10 15 0		
30 0 30	19 5 0	24 0 0	18 0 0	16 5 0		
25 1 5	18 5 0	25 0 0	18 15 0	14 10 0		
11 1 23	7 0 0	12 3 0	9 0 0	7 0 0		
7 3 7	8 5 0	5 15 0	5 11 0	3 13 0		
15 1 30	11 0 0	15 5 0	10 10 0	7 7 0		
6 3 5	4 15 0	5 5 0	4 4 0	3 3 0		
14 1 37	6 15 0	10 14 1	9 0 0	7 5 0		
21 3 29	22 8 0	25 15 3	28 0 0	21 0 0		
43 0 10	24 15 0	24 5 0	24 0 0	18 10 0		
15 0 10	Unascertained	13 13 0	10 0 0	9 0 0		
11 0 0	8 0 0	10 5 0	8 5 0	5 5 0		

GROUND STATUTORY TERM.

COUNTY OF

Name of Assistant Commissioners by whom Cases were decided.	Record Number.	Date of Order.	Name of Tenant.	Name of Landlord.	Townland.
Assistant Commissioners—		1897.			
J. H. Rowe (Legal). F. O'Callaghan. L. Crinket.	215	March 17,	Hugh Coyle,	George E. Smith,	Anthony,
	213	„	John Kiernan,	do.	do.
	220	„	John Sheridan,	do.	do.
	219	„	John Leddy,	do.	do.
	265	„	Thomas Brady,	Rev. F. Fitzpatrick,	Turlalands Lower,
	263	„	Patrick O'Reilly,	do.	do.
	231	„	Michael Cahey,	do.	do.
	235	„	Patrick Smith,	do.	do.
	262	„	John Daly,	do.	do.
	287	„	Thomas Rudden,	do.	do.
	268	„	Pat Daly, Junior,	do.	do.
	254	„	John Tierney,	do.	do.
	227	„	James Brady,	do.	do.
	636	„	Elizabeth Rudden, Ltd. Admin. of Patrick Rudden.	do.	do.
					Total,

COUNTY OF

Name of Assistant Commissioners by whom Cases were decided.	Record Number.	Date of Order.	Name of Tenant.	Name of Landlord.	Townland.
Assistant Commissioners—					
D. Tierney (Legal). G. H. Millis. J. W. Barlow.	355	March 9,	James Friel,	Charles E. Harvey,	Ballymorey,
	779	„	James Boner,	do.	do.
	371	„	William M'Keogue,	do.	do.
	649	„	William Lee,	do.	do.
	627	„	James Lee,	do.	do.
	690	„	Robert M'Keogue,	do.	do.
	349	„	John Ramsey,	do.	do.
	130	„	Betty Travers,	do.	do.
	611	„	Bridget Doherty,	do.	do.
	177	„	Denis M'Loughlin,	Courtenay H. Newton,	Ballymorey,
	78	„	George Baldrick,	Thompson M. M'Clintock,	Aghamore,
	329	„	James Doherty,	do.	do.
	143	„	Hannah Casey, Ltd. Admin. of Anthony Casey, deceased.	Mrs. John Ferguson,	Carrickahulion,
	271	„	Thomas Wright,	Leslie Alexander,	Tullydish Lower,
	800	„	Do.,	do.	Tullydish Upper,

CAVAN—continued.

Extent of Holding Square	Poor Law Valuation.	Rent of Holding prior to creation of First Statutory Term.	Judicial Rent for First Statutory Term.	Judicial Rent for Second Statutory Term.	Observations.	Value of Tenancy.
A. R. P.	£ s. d.	£ s. d.	£ s. d.	£ s. d.		£ s. d.
14 5 6	9 15 0	11 15 0	10 7 6	8 10 0		
17 0 32	9 0 0	12 0 0	10 12 5	8 5 0		
16 1 9	11 5 0	13 7 0	11 5 0	9 15 0		
18 3 5	13 17 0	16 6 0	13 10 0	10 0 0		
15 1 14	8 7 0	10 14 6	7 12 0	6 6 0		
21 0 1	5 18 0	6 7 5	8 10 0	5 0 0		
18 0 12	16 15 0	17 4 0	20 0 0	15 0 0		
18 1 7	7 5 0	10 13 0	5 9 0	5 15 0		
18 3 10	7 5 0	9 16 5	7 0 0	5 17 0		
30 0 60	10 8 0	14 17 5	11 0 0	9 5 0		
10 3 15	5 15 0	6 17 5	5 5 0	4 18 0		
14 3 20	11 10 0	13 9 6	10 5 0	9 0 0		
15 0 4	7 10 0	10 15 0	5 0 0	5 10 0		
19 0 9	10 5 0	15 13 6	11 0 0	9 0 0		
1,331 1 1	764 10 0	1,043 10 11	623 1 6	631 16 6		

DONEGAL.

65 0 0	5 0 0	7 10 0	6 0 0	4 14 0		
16 1 15	5 18 0	7 3 6	5 10 0	6 6 0		
13 1 19	7 0 0	5 10 0	6 10 0	1 15 0		
19 3 15	9 0 0	19 9 0	8 16 0	5 15 0		
13 0 23	5 5 0		9 16 0	5 0 0		
72 6 13	5 5 0	5 10 0	7 10 0	4 19 0		
16 1 14	5 0 0	6 11 0	5 0 0	4 6 0		
90 1 0	11 0 0	16 9 6	16 0 0	9 17 0		
87 3 21	15 15 0	16 0 0	14 5 0	10 17 0		
44 6 17	12 0 0	17 10 0	12 0 0	9 17 0		
16 3 0	11 15 0	15 3 3	10 15 0	5 13 0		
5 6 6	5 15 0	13 0 0	6 0 0	5 10 0		
91 1 0	25 10 0	20 16 0	23 0 0	23 6 0		
177 3 7	54 9 9	44 16 6	31 10 0	25 0 0		
7 1 0	2 16 0	6 0 0	5 15 0	8 17 0		

IRISH LAND COMMISSION.

SECOND STATUTORY TERM.

Names of Assistant Commissioners by whom Cases were decided.	Record Number.	Date of Order.	Name of Tenant.	Name of Landlord.	Townland.
Assistant Commissioners:— D. Towns (Legal). G. H. Miller. J. W. Barber.		**1897.**			
	323	March 8,	Daniel Sheward,	John Scott,	Tabanne,
	842	,,	John Barr,	Leslie Alexander,	Revlin,
	79	,,	James Doherty,	do.	Tullyarvan,
	80	,,	Daniel M'Kinney,	do.	do.
	83	,,	Neal Doherty,	do.	do.
	333	,,	Edward Doherty,	Daniel O'Doherty,	Ballygowan,
	181	,,	John Doherty, Ld. Admor. of Michael A. Doherty,	William R. Harte,	Ardmalin,
	344	Jan. 22,	John Doherty,	Guernsey H. Newton,	Ballyamone,
	333	March 3,	Robert M'Neill,	J. M. G. Grove,	Rakirril,
	338	,,	David M'Clay,	do.	do.
	340	,,	Daniel Cromm,	do.	do.
	384	,,	Robert M'Nutt,	do.	do.
	340	,,	Wm. Hamer, Adm. of David Reaton, decd.	do.	Raymoghy,
	343	March 8,	James Turner,	Thomas Colquhoun,	Rossbunion,
	343	,,	Joseph Tinney,	do.	do.
	344	,,	James Mills,	do.	do.
	163	March 9,	Mary Doherty,	William R. Harte,	Ardmalin,
	165	,,	Margaret Doherty,	do.	do.
	175	,,	Daniel M'Laughlin,	do.	do.
	177	,,	John H. Doherty,	do.	do.
	185	,,	James Doherty, junr.,	do.	do.
	139	,,	Patrick R. Doherty,	do.	do.
	187	,,	John Doherty (Pat's)	do.	do.
	143	,,	Neal Doherty,	do.	do.
	94	March 11,	Hugh Kearney,	David J. Gilliland,	Slestin,
	77	March 9,	Anne M'Donald,	Ernest Cochrane,	Carlebangh,
	148	,,	Sally M'Gaughan,	do.	Glenmakim,
	221	,,	John Canidy,	do.	Trillick,
	343	,,	James Doherty,	do.	Laddier,
	192	,,	Andrew M'Laughlin,	do.	do.
	209	,,	Daniel M'Laughlin,	Charles R. Harvey,	Monnagh,
	125	,,	Do.,	do.	do.
	210	,,	John J. Doherty,	do.	Garryerrigan,

DONEGAL—continued.

Amount of Existing Rents.	Poor Law Valuation.	Rent of Holding prior to creation of First Statutory Term.	Judicial Rent for First Statutory Term.	Judicial Rent for Second Statutory Term.	Observations.	Value of Tenancy.
£ s. d.	£ s. d.	£ s. d.	£ s. d.	£ s. d.		£ s. d.
15 0 23	18 5 0	24 0 0	23 0 0	11 10 0		
24 2 15	9 5 0	18 5 9	10 10 0	9 8 0		
23 1 24	7 10 0	13 12 8	7 10 0	6 11 0		
9 1 9	4 6 0	6 6 0	3 5 0	3 10 0		
13 3 13	7 10 0	6 13 9	3 10 9	5 3 0		
11 0 16	6 15 0	5 5 0	3 12 0	3 3 0		
13 1 13	4 0 0	5 10 0	4 5 0	3 1 0		
17 2 23	6 6 0	7 12 0	4 3 0	4 4 0	By consent	
11 3 30	7 0 0	9 0 0	4 0 0	5 3 0	do.	
21 3 4	5 5 0	11 0 0	5 0 0	6 14 0	do.	
30 0 9	11 5 0	15 0 0	11 0 0	8 7 0	do.	
23 1 0	6 4 0	6 5 0	4 10 0	3 16 6	do.	
39 1 30	40 10 0	53 13 9	40 0 0	40 0 6	do.	
36 1 30	30 0 0	34 14 0	30 10 0	16 8 0	do.	
23 3 6	24 15 0	27 14 0	26 0 0	20 16 0	do.	
33 1 30	30 0 0	23 3 0	19 0 0	16 4 0	do.	
14 3 23	4 0 0	6 6 0	4 3 0	3 15 0		
17 3 14	4 10 0	6 1 9	5 5 4	3 16 0		
13 0 30	4 0 0	4 17 10	4 6 3	2 17 6		
15 1 0	4 15 0	5 13 10	5 15 9	3 10 0		
7 3 21	4 10 0	5 16 6	4 6 6	3 17 0		
9 0 33	3 15 0	6 10 0	3 0 0	7 7 6		
9 1 33	4 5 0	6 0 0	4 16 9	3 16 0		
13 0 13	3 10 0	4 13 9	5 1 0	2 15 0		
43 0 13	26 0 0	23 14 6	21 0 0	19 5 0		
47 2 4	34 15 0	37 9 6	35 0 0	23 15 6		
43 3 14	9 15 0	12 0 9	12 0 0	10 14 0		
99 0 14	16 0 0	16 1 0	16 20 0	14 15 0		
38 7 33	6 3 0	6 4 7	5 16 0	4 16 0		
47 3 23	19 3 0	71 0 0	15 10 0	13 0 0		
6 9 0	9 15 0	3 10 0	3 0 0	2 10 6		
7 3 33	6 0 0	5 10 0	4 7 6	3 16 0		
36 0 14	13 15 0	16 18 0	15 0 0	9 4 0		

1

SECOND STATUTORY TERM.

COUNTY OF

Names of Assistant Commissioners by whom Cases were decided.	Record Number.	Date of Order.	Name of Tenant.	Name of Landlord.	Townland.
Assistant Commissioners—		1897.			
D. TICKEY (Legal). R. SPROULE. J. M. KELLY.	6	March 8,	Unby Bradey, ...	Mrs. Elizabeth F. M. C. Cockrane and another.	Turc, —
	41	,,	Patrick M'Laughlin,	do.	Castlequarter, —
	40	,,	William Cunningham,	do. — ...	Magheralug, —
	39	,,	Mary O'Donnell, —	do. — ...	do. —
	31	,,	James M'Arthur, ...	Lord Templemore, ...	Spamoge, —
	98	,,	James Robinson, ...	do. — ...	Toolan, —
	7	,,	John Stevenson, —	do. — ...	Ballikine Lower, —
	2	,,	Mary Brodie, —	do. — ...	Drumanoyne, —
	204	,,	William Foyn, —	George K. Gifford, —	Carrabegh, —
	202	,,	Hugh M'Cann, ...	do. — —	do. —
	206	,,	Edward M'Guialn, Ltd. Admr. of Hugh M'Guialn, decd.	do. — —	do. —
	207	,,	Do. — —	do. — —	do. —
	16	,,	Sarah M'Loughlin, ...	E. F. M. C. Cockrane and another.	Castlequarter, —
	14	,,	James M'Cael, —	do. — ...	Turc, —
	16	,,	Fanny Margey, —	do. — —	do. —
	14	,,	Mary Anne Styne, —	do. ... —	do. —
	18	,,	John M'Colgan, —	do. — —	Drumaballen, —
	13	,,	William Lyons, —	do. — —	do. —
	11	,,	John Doherty, —	do. — ...	do. —
	10	,,	James M'Kendrick, —	do. — —	do. —
	8	,,	Matthew Ferguson, —	do. — —	Turc, —
C. H. TICKING (Legal). W. S. HUNT.	372	Feb. 15,	John O'Flagherty, ...	William M'Granty, —	Magheragh and another.
	176	,,	John Hegarty, ...	do. — —	Magheragh.
	176	,,	Do. — —	do. — —	Magheragh and another.
	373	,,	John Cairns, ...	do. — —	Carrollton, —
C. H. TICKING (Legal). R. H. PRINGLE. J. A. SMITH.	441	March 22,	Patrick M'Closky, ...	R. S. Chatterton and another, Trustees of Wm. Young.	Gorradowy, —
	37	,,	John Donnell, —	Sir Samuel H. Hayes, Bart.	Callan, —
	751	,,	Mary Healy, Ltd. Admr. of Pk. Healy.	R. S. Chatterton and another, Trustees of Wm. Young.	Gorradowy, —
	443	,,	James Bradley, —	do. — ...	do. —

SECOND STATUTORY TERM.

DONEGAL—*continued.*

Amount of Holding Rents.	Poor Law Valuation.	Rent of Holding prior to fixing of First Statutory Term.	Judicial Rent for First Statutory Term.	Judicial Rent for Second Statutory Term.	Observations.	Value of Tenancy.
£ s. d.	£ s. d.	£ s. d.	£ s. d.	£ s. d.		£ s. d.
16 0 18	15 16 6	17 13 5	13 10 0	8 5 6		
71 0 90	89 5 0	53 3 2	23 10 0	17 5 0		
17 3 27	11 0 0	15 3 3	17 0 0	12 5 0		
40 1 53	33 5 0	54 0 0	34 0 0	25 0 0		
174 1 30	99 13 9	117 0 0	72 0 0	61 10 0		
155 0 0	76 15 0	78 0 0	49 0 0	40 0 0		
114 3 0	48 5 0	54 15 0	73 10 0	50 0 0		
10 1 35	13 10 0	16 0 0	10 10 0	8 10 0		
13 1 0	9 10 0	19 17 0	10 10 0	4 15 0		
10 0 10	8 8 0	10 5 0	7 10 0	5 5 0		
8 3 10	3 5 0	3 15 0	4 15 0	5 15 0		
16 3 60	6 5 0	10 10 0	8 10 5	5 11 0		
13 5 0	21 0 0	23 10 0	15 10 0	13 5 0		
28 5 0	13 5 0	14 10 0	11 5 0	8 15 0		
15 0 5	10 0 0	16 6 10	17 0 0	9 10 0		
11 1 29	14 5 0	16 6 10	13 5 0	9 5 0		
8 3 0	5 15 0	6 5 0	4 15 0	3 0 0	And 5th of 50s. 2s. undivided mountain.	
121 5 15	15 0 0	15 5 5	19 0 0	9 0 0		
8 3 12	8 15 0	8 8 0	4 15 0	3 0 0	And 5th of 60s. 2s. undivided mountain.	
50 0 0	13 0 0	16 15 0	11 0 0	8 5 0	And 5th of 50s. 2s. undivided mountain.	
15 3 10	20 0 0	13 6 10	13 5 0	10 0 0		
41 3 25	40 10 0	56 5 0	44 0 0	33 0 0	By consent.	
48 0 0	77 10 5	100 0 0	77 10 0	68 5 0	do.	
54 3 9	80 5 0	43 14 5	59 0 0	54 0 0	do.	
51 0 0	17 10 0	37 5 2	18 10 0	14 15 0	do.	
341 1 50	23 0 0	81 0 0	80 10 0	17 5 7		
20 3 10	7 15 0	9 3 6	8 0 0	8 17 1		
64 0 0	5 5 0	13 13 10	10 5 0	10 5 0		
40 0 0	7 0 0	9 15 5	5 15 0	4 15 1		

IRISH LAND COMMISSION.

SECOND STATUTORY TERM.

COUNTY OF

Name of Assistant Commissioners by whom Case was decided.	Record Number.	Date of Order.	Name of Tenant.	Name of Landlord.	Townland.
Assistant Commissioners—		1887.			
C. H. Tennant (Legal). R. H. Prendlis. J. A. Smith.	463	March 22,	Ellen M'Loughlin, ...	R. S. Chatterton and anor., Trustees of Wm. Young.	Curraduay, ...
	470	„	Andrew Birney, ...	Col. Charles H. Knox, ...	Cornish, ...
	333	„	Samuel Woods, ...	do. ...	Ballybofey, ...
	112	„	James Reilly, ...	do. ...	do. ...
					Total, ...

COUNTY OF

Assistant Commissioners—		1887.			
W. F. Bailey (Legal). H. Byrne. S. G. Williams.	500	March 16,	Samuel Arnold, ...	John Joseph White, ...	Doagary, ...
	509	„	Robert Cronin, ...	do. ...	do. ...
	516	„	Henry Stevenson, ...	do. ...	Tullyner, ...
	399	„	Sarah Matchett, ...	do. ...	do. ...
	408	„	Do. ...	do. ...	do. ...
	510	„	Robert Cronin, ...	do. ...	do. ...
	339	„	James Hamilton, ...	do. ...	do. ...
	353	„	Robert J. Hills, ...	do. ...	do. ...
	594	„	John Curran, ...	do. ...	do. ...
	587	„	Do. ...	do. ...	do. ...
	594	„	John Curran & anor., ...	do. ...	do. ...
	596	„	John Radcliffe, ...	do. ...	do. ...
	597	„	William Moss, ...	do. ...	do. ...
	388	„	David Kernaghan, ...	do. ...	do. ...
	398	„	James Matchett, ...	do. ...	do. ...
	391	„	Andrew Pinkerton, ...	do. ...	do. ...
	548	„	William Thompson, ...	do. ...	Doagary, ...
	519	„	James Porter, ...	do. ...	do. ...
	390	„	William J. Hamilton, ...	do. ...	do. ...
	372	„	Andrew Porter, ...	do. ...	do. ...
	545	„	James Hughes, ...	do. ...	do. ...
	507	„	Robert M'Clements, ...	do. ...	Cahanamore, ...
	537	„	James Hamilton, ...	do. ...	Doagary, ...
	538	„	Joseph M'Cullagh, ...	do. ...	Ballydawn, ...
	544	„	James Hughes, ...	do. ...	Doagary, ...

SECOND STATUTORY TERM.

DONEGAL.—*continued*.

Extent of Holding. Roods.	Poor Law Valuation.	Rent of Holding prior to creation of First Statutory Term.	Judicial Rent for First Statutory Term.	Judicial Rent for Second Statutory Term.	Observations.	Value of Tenancy.
A. R. P.	£ s. d.	£ s. d.	£ s. d.	£ s. d.		£ s. d.
17 0 0	3 13 0	6 0 0	8 10 0	3 4 6		
7 3 15	9 10 0	9 4 6	8 14 2	4 2 10		
14 6 20	50 10 0	23 16 10	16 16 0	11 13 0		
1 2 0	6 0 0	7 0 6	6 13 6	5 16 10		
108 2 10	1,206 17 0	1,612 13 7	1,585 3 0	855 2 10		

DOWN.

13 1 10	16 0 0	16 6 0	14 0 0	10 0 6		
33 3 13	37 16 0	43 17 8	34 7 6	27 0 0		
4 3 6	9 10 0	11 4 0	9 13 11	6 17 6		
2 3 0	9 5 0	9 16 0	9 0 0	6 5 0		
13 6 6	16 16 0	16 2 2	13 10 0	10 10 0		
11 1 30	34 13 0	61 17 6	31 0 0	78 10 0		
1 1 30	6 0 0	6 0 0	6 10 0	3 5 0		
7 6 0	6 6 0	6 16 2	7 16 0	6 17 6		
10 0 86	34 3 0	39 1 1	31 10 0	34 13 0		
16 3 7	14 0 0	20 9 0	17 16 0	18 10 0		
11 1 16	13 10 0	13 4 4	13 4 6	9 0 0		
7 6 0	13 0 0	16 7 6	11 30 0	7 0 6		
6 0 9	6 5 0	6 6 0	8 8 0	3 16 0		
11 0 36	16 5 0	16 11 10	14 11 10	6 5 0		
21 2 25	34 10 0	26 6 0	23 0 0	16 0 0		
6 3 23	13 0 0	11 11 0	10 10 0	7 10 0		
79 0 23	31 10 0	31 16 0	33 0 0	22 0 0		
61 0 16	61 6 0	63 3 1	46 10 0	34 0 0		
21 1 60	26 6 0	26 16 1	21 0 0	17 0 0		
37 3 23	31 0 0	36 3 7	33 0 0	12 10 0		
13 2 22	13 16 6	16 7 10	14 0 0	9 16 0		
34 1 23	33 10 0	43 6 10	37 10 0	36 0 0		
10 3 12	23 15 0	23 15 11	23 10 0	16 0 0		
13 1 23	10 16 0	16 0 4	12 16 0	10 0 0		
16 1 36	11 10 0	21 9 6	20 16 0	14 0 0		

IRISH LAND COMMISSION.

SECOND STATUTORY TERM.

Name of Assistant Commissioners by whom Cases were decided.	Record Number.	Date of Court.	Name of Tenant.	Name of Landlord.	Townland.
Assistant Commissioners—		1897.			
W. F. Bailey (Legal). A. Byrne. S. G. Williams.	414	March 18,	Mary MacGl,	John Joseph White,	Ballybawn,
	266	,,	Wm. Rhodds,	do.	do.
	408	,,	James Leehey,	do.	Colmarmon,
	418	,,	James M'Knight,	do.	do.
	407	,,	David Stewart,	J. C. Stewart,	Cumlerumna,
	448	,,	Bernard Neill,	J. A. Knox,	Drumkineel,
	443	,,	Susan Neill, Admx. of Catherine Rooney, deceased,	Rev. B. D. Kent,	do.
	457	,,	Wm. John Rooney,	do.	do.
	456	,,	Patrick M'Cann,	do.	do.
	441	,,	John Rooney,	do.	do.
	782	,,	John Young,	James Birch,	Ballyroney,
	446	,,	George Wilson,	Mrs. Sarah Nicholson,	Drumtemagh,
	810	,,	Ellen M'Dowell,	A. B. Moncaley,	Derrylough and others,
	1087	March 20,	Andrew Kennedy,	F. A. Crommellin,	Cortny Hill,
	1048	,,	Edward M'Brear,	do.	Cortny Hill and others,
W. F. Bailey (Legal). W. Williams. G. M. Harvey.	604	March 18,	Daniel Rooney,	Michael M'Courville and another,	Edentrumly,
	659	,,	Do.	do.	do.
	333	,,	Patrick Rooney,	do.	do.
	328	,,	John Rooney,	do.	do.
	331	,,	Nicholas Woods,	do.	do.
	330	,,	Arthur Rooney,	do.	do.
	339	,,	Daniel Meehin,	do.	do.
	826	,,	Owen Downey,	do.	do.
	327	,,	Peter Rooney (Carmichael),	do.	do.
	326	,,	Michael Rooney,	do.	do.
	338	,,	Mary O'Neill,	do.	do.
	334	,,	John Rooney,	do.	do.
	332	,,	Peter Oridinan,	do.	do.
	337	,,	Hugh M'Genny,	do.	do.

SECOND STATUTORY TERM.

DOWN—*continued.*

Amount of Holding Down.	Poor Law Valuation.	Rent of Holding prior to creation of First Statutory Term	Judicial Rent for First Statutory Term.	Judicial Rent for Second Statutory Term.	Observations	Value of Tenancy.
£ s. d.	£ s. d.	£ s. d.	£ s. d.	£ s. d.		£ s. d.
13 1 35	14 10 0	17 7 9	13 10 0	10 0 0		
6 0 13	4 5 0	6 11 3	6 0 0	4 0 0		
4 3 10	4 5 0	5 10 0	4 12 0	3 13 8		
10 1 80	10 0 0	13 15 0	11 0 0	8 10 0		
14 0 13	13 0 0	16 16 9	14 0 0	13 0 0		
15 1 85	16 0 0	27 0 0	20 0 0	11 0 0		
6 3 10	7 10 0		6 5 0	4 17 6		
		31 0 0				
13 3 30	16 0 0		17 15 0	13 5 0		
13 1 30	13 10 0	17 10 0	13 0 0	10 6 0		
5 3 27	6 10 0	8 0 0	6 10 0	4 10 0		
30 3 34	36 15 0	33 7 8	29 0 0	23 0 0		
16 3 35	21 0 0	35 0 0	25 0 0	18 10 0		
23 0 0	21 0 0	43 0 0	29 0 0	21 0 0		
17 1 9	31 5 0	30 7 8	30 0 0	16 16 0	By consent.	
6 0 30	5 13 0	13 3 0	7 10 0	6 0 0	do.	
6 1 0	5 10 6	8 0 0	4 0 0	3 9 0	With right of mountain grazing.	
10 1 30	6 15 0	7 6 8	5 5 0	4 15 0	do.	
30 0 8	13 0 0	19 7 6	16 0 0	10 3 0	do.	
3 3 30	3 0 0	6 3 9	3 6 0	3 0 0		
6 1 30	11 0 0	16 11 0	5 0 0	3 13 3		
16 0 10	16 15 0	17 16 0	13 10 0	5 5 0		
17 1 5	13 10 0	19 15 6	16 0 0	9 15 0	do.	
15 0 35	17 5 0	21 16 10	17 10 0	13 5 0	do.	
33 0 0	6 5 0	9 15 0	6 10 0	5 10 0	do.	
13 3 27	5 5 0	10 12 6	5 5 0	5 0 0	do.	
5 0 0	8 10 0	3 10 0	3 10 0	1 17 6		
11 1 30	11 5 0	11 11 0	10 5 0	7 10 0		
7 3 33	6 10 0	7 10 0	6 0 0	5 7 6	do.	
6 1 35	3 0 0	3 10 0	3 17 8	6 13 0	do.	
9 0 30	6 5 0	7 10 0	3 10 0	4 12 0	do.	
13 1 30	9 0 0	10 0 5	5 5 0	6 11 0	do.	
14 3 30	13 5 0	12 10 0	10 5 0	7 0 0		

72 IRISH LAND COMMISSION.

SECOND STATUTORY TERM.

COUNTY OF

Name of Assistant Commissioner by whom Court was decided.	Record Number.	Date of Order.	Name of Tenant.	Name of Landlord.	Townland.
Antecoaps Courts (continued)—		1897.			
W. F. Bailey (Legal). W. Wallace. G. M. Harvey.	315	March 13.	Peter Ramsey (Carrmore).	Richard M'Onville and another.	Educrossina,
	317	„	Do.	do.	do.
	316	„	Arthur Ramsey,	do.	do.
	319	„	John Small,	do.	do.
	314	„	James M'Geary,	do.	do.
	313	„	John O'Rorke,	do.	do.
	318	„	James Murphy,	do.	do.
	321	„	Constantine Ramsey,	do.	Tattanalurry,
	278	„	Patrick O'Neill, sen.,	do.	do.
	370	„	Peter Kane,	do.	do.
	368	„	Thomas Kane,	do.	do.
	369	„	Owen M'Geary,	do.	do.
	368	„	Patrick O'Neill, jun.,	do.	do.
	365	„	Charles Grant,	do.	do.
	402	„	Bernard Duran,	do.	do.
	338	March 8.	Thomas Merron,	(General Andrew Nugent),	Craigmaddin and another.
W. F. Bailey (Legal). C. W. Thompson. D. O'C. Dalmall.	389	March 9.	Daniel Cliff, & anor.,	Captain John Ruxton,	Ballyrunning,
	530	„	Richard Hughes,	do.	do.
	462	„	Mary Moorhead,	do.	Ballyphiph,
	353	„	Ellen Smith,	Hugh Savage,	Ballywalden,
	351	„	Patrick Smith,	do.	do.
	451	„	Catherine Boyd and another,	Major-Gen. W. E. Montgomery,	Kirkistown,
	457	„	William Clarke,	Gertrude Higginson and others,	Ballysacurna,
	446	„	William Savage,	do.	do.
	448	„	William J. Long,	do.	do.
	450	„	Emily Martin,	J. B. Raphael and another,	Ballyroman,
	518A	„	William T. M'Gibbon,	do.	do.
	518B	„	Phebe J. Kirkpatrick,	do.	do.
	517	„	James Smith,	do.	do.
	618	„	William Dempster,	James Hamm,	Glen,
	680	„	Robert Moore, jun.,	do.	do.

Printed and re-digitised by the University of Southampton Library Digitisation Unit

SECOND STATUTORY TERM.

DOWN—continued.

Extent of Holding.	Poor Law Valuation.	Rent of Holding prior to exertion of First Statutory Term.	Judicial Rent for First Statutory Term.	Judicial Rent for Second Statutory Term.	Observations.	Value of Tenancy.
a. r. p.	£ s. d.	£ s. d.	£ s. d.	£ s. d.		£ s. d.
2 3 34	7 5 0	10 18 5	7 5 0	5 5 0	With right of mountain grazing.	
1 1 0	1 10 0		1 0 0	0 15 0		
15 1 0	0 10 0	27 8 10	10 10 0	8 3 0	Holding divided since exertion of First Statutory Term.	
14 0 0	13 0 0		11 0 0	5 10 0		
10 1 30	5 10 0	6 1 0	5 0 0	5 10 0	Right of grazing on mountain.	
1 3 15	6 15 0	7 0 0	6 0 0	4 5 0		
4 0 0	4 0 0	6 13 3	4 13 3	2 13 6		
11 5 33	4 5 0	—	6 10 0	5 4 0	Holding changed since exertion of First Statutory Term. Former rent of entire holding, £14 16s. 11d.	
7 0 34	6 5 0	6 0 0	6 10 0	5 3 0		
5 8 1	3 10 0	4 3 6	3 5 0	1 10 0		
13 1 24	6 5 0	11 4 7	6 15 0	6 10 0		
3 3 17	3 10 0	3 11 1	2 15 0	1 13 0		
7 3 3	6 15 0	6 0 6	4 15 0	6 15 0	Right of grazing as heretofore.	
3 3 14	6 10 0	9 15 10	6 10 0	3 0 0		
6 1 4	3 0 0	3 16 3	2 17 6	1 17 0	Right of grazing as heretofore.	
14 2 15	36 10 0	38 19 6	64 0 0	22 17 5		
22 1 27	36 10 0	46 17 4	38 20 0	14 10 0		
14 1 15	35 10 0	32 11 10	26 0 0	15 5 0		
49 3 37	9 15 0	6 11 0	7 10 0	5 12 0		
4 0 17	5 15 0	5 14 7	5 17 5	5 14 0		
47 1 24	20 0 0	21 4 9	18 0 0	13 0 0		
1 3 34	6 0 0	5 5 3	5 10 0	4 15 0		
14 0 20	—	55 5 0	22 0 0	27 5 0		
17 5 0	15 10 0	18 5 0	14 10 0	10 0 0		
60 0 0	55 0 0	70 10 0	55 0 0	33 10 0		
54 0 5	56 5 0	75 5 0	67 3 3	37 0 0		
57 2 11	67 0 0	78 0 4	50 5 6	41 5 0		
34 3 15	51 0 0	46 9 3	15 17 2	39 10 0		
18 1 13	37 10 0	40 3 10	50 15 5	31 5 0		
5 0 33	34 5 0	50 19 0	22 5 0	15 5 5		
71 3 6	23 0 0	51 11 3	18 0 0	15 5 0		

IRISH LAND COMMISSION.

SECOND STATUTORY TERM.

Names of Assistant Commissioners by whom Cases were decided.	Record Number.	Date of Order.	Name of Tenant.	Name of Landlord.	Townland.
Assistant Commissioners—		1897.			
W. F. BAILEY (Legal). G. W. THOMPSON. D. O'C. DOUGLAS.	539	March 8,	Robert Moore, jr.,	James Hewson,	Clen,
	538	"	Ellen Harper,	do.	Tullyroany,
	444	"	George M'Connell and another,	do.	Clen,
	537	"	Robert Wilson,	General Andrew Nugent,	Ballybrannigan and another,
	540	"	Thomas Maxwell,	do.	Ballymoriny,
	341	"	Hugh Wilson,	do.	Ballybrannigan,
	342	"	Do.	do.	Corvey,
	343	"	Thomas Maxwell,	do.	do.
	543	"	Do.	do.	do.
	450	"	William Logan,	do.	Ballyward,
	161	"	Patrick Dynan,	do.	Ballyroaney,
	344	"	Patrick Quinn,	do.	do.
	551	"	John Smith,	do.	Ballyward,
	461	"	Lizzie Lennon,	do.	Threehilly,
	459	"	Phelin J. Kirkpatrick,	do.	Correagh,
	401	"	James Shanks,	do.	Ballyfannin,
	547	"	George M'Robb,	do.	Kavanagh,
	544	"	Do.	do.	do.
	399	"	Thomas Keating,	do.	Turn,
	398	"	James Mann,	do.	do.
	431	"	Richard M'Robb,	do.	Craigroahan,
	458	"	Lizzie Lennon,	do.	do.
	552	March 15,	Hugh Mawrory,	Lord De Ros,	Correagh,
	686	"	Richard Doris,	Lord Bangor,	Ballynordan,
	428	"	Wm. M'Collough and another,	Pardo A. Klein,	Ballywillin,
	587	"	James M'Keown,	do.	do.
	526	"	John M'Cann,	do.	do.
	459	"	Ralph M'Carten,	do.	do.
	814	"	John M'Elroy,	Francis Hewson,	Toye,
	145	"	George M'Connell,	do.	do.
	800	"	James M'Cun,	Captain Sinton,	Ballingrum,
	412	"	William Martin,	R. K. Boyd,	Ballylenagh,
	411	"	Do.	do.	do.
	1784	"	William Newell,	Earl of Kilmorey,	Burngh,

SECOND STATUTORY TERM.

DOWN—*continued.*

Amount of Holding Rents.	Poor Law Valuation.	Rent of Holding prior to creation of First Statutory Term.	Judicial Rent for First Statutory Term.	Judicial Rent for Second Statutory Term.	Observations.	Value of Tenancy.
£ s. d.	£ s. d.	£ s. d.	£ s. d.	£ s. d.		£ s. d.
18 1 10	51 0 0	53 18 0	58 0 0	18 4 8		
13 0 11	31 5 0	37 16 0	34 0 0	19 6 0		
60 0 0	66 5 0	67 8 0	57 10 0	34 5 0		
13 1 23	18 10 0	34 4 0	20 0 0	16 0 0		
24 0 4	18 10 0	23 18 8	19 0 0	13 15 0		
34 1 54	37 0 0	28 14 0	30 10 0	21 17 8		
16 1 15	13 0 0	17 7 6	15 0 0	13 7 8		
8 1 10	—	7 8 4	7 8 6	8 0 0		
33 0 31	30 10 0	37 16 0	33 0 0	61 14 0		
36 3 0	34 15 0	34 16 2	31 0 0	20 8 0		
30 8 36	—	} 67 4 0 {	37 0 0	37 0 0	} Holding subdivided since creation of First Statutory Term.	
9 1 23	13 0 0		9 15 0	6 10 0		
33 3 11	36 0 0	37 8 3	24 10 8	17 5 0		
17 1 54	37 15 0	68 13 0	34 4 0	37 10 0		
43 3 54	64 5 0	63 5 6	50 0 0	33 14 0		
67 1 18	76 10 0	73 7 10	63 0 0	38 14 0		
85 1 19	86 0 0	81 0 0	68 0 0	37 18 0		
64 0 31	43 0 0	35 0 0	30 15 0	34 4 0		
61 5 0	37 0 0	26 17 5	34 17 8	18 4 0		
31 3 5	62 15 0	54 0 0	60 10 0	36 15 0		
73 0 37	67 10 0	71 7 0	61 0 0	42 5 0		
5 1 14	7 15 0	7 8 0	7 5 0	6 5 0		
11 3 25	18 0 0	16 16 0	9 0 0	5 0 0		
34 3 0	26 10 0	37 0 0	31 0 0	13 10 0		
16 3 8	13 5 0	14 8 8	12 0 0	6 16 0		
14 8 0	14 5 0	20 6 0	16 0 0	11 0 0		
11 1 0	10 6 0	13 0 0	9 13 0	7 6 0		
16 1 16	14 15 0	19 14 10	18 18 0	10 0 0		
61 0 10	66 0 0	85 15 0	67 0 0	61 14 0		
6 5 38	11 10 0	11 0 6	10 15 0	8 0 0		
63 1 23	68 10 0	68 8 0	65 0 0	37 17 8		
17 1 7	16 10 0	23 16 8	16 10 0	11 17 0		
64 1 37	68 15 0	63 5 8	72 11 0	48 0 0		
51 3 30	58 15 0	67 5 6	41 0 0	33 10 0	By consent.	

IRISH LAND COMMISSION.

SECOND STATUTORY TERM.

COUNTY OF

Names of Assistant Commissioners by whom Cases were decided.	Record Number	Date of Order	Name of Tenant.	Name of Landlord.	Townland.
Assistant Commissioners— W. F. BAILEY (Legal), W. H. O. BYRNE, J. ———		1877.			
	569	March 24,	Alexander Black,	Rev. R. J. Smyth,	Ballyhoyd,
	570	"	George Jess,	do.	do.
	571	"	John H. Johnston,	do.	do.
	572	"	Thomas Ferguson,	do.	do.
	441	"	Robert Brok,	do.	do.
	552	"	Samuel Campbell,	do.	do.
	553	"	William Crawford,	do.	do.
	554	"	Samuel Wilson,	do.	do.
	555	"	Thomas Tate,	do.	do.
	556	"	George Jess,	do.	do.
	557	"	James Boyd,	do.	do.
	558	"	Samuel J. Ervin,	do.	do.
	559	"	James Cairns,	do.	do.
	563	"	James M'Keever,	do.	do.
	560	"	James Magill,	do.	do.
	562	"	Mark Hamilton,	do.	do.
	561	"	Thomas Ferguson,	do.	do.
	469	"	James Tollerton,	R. J. Hunter & ors., Trustees of George J. Hunter.	Drumena,
	496	"	Robert M'Master,	do.	do.
	497	"	Do.	do.	do.
	498	"	James Patterson,	do.	do.
	433	"	Bryan M'Kay,	do.	do.
	464	"	William J. Smith,	do.	do.
	577	"	Hugh Rice,	John Hart,	Ballyquintin,
	575	"	John Rice,	do.	do.
	578	"	Agnes Rice,	do.	do.
	579	"	Robert Lindsay,	do.	do.
	576	"	Agnes Rice,	do.	do.
					Total,

COUNTY OF

Assistant Commissioners— A. R. Merriman ?, A. S. Drape.					
	67	Feb. 27,	Andrew M'Cashey,	Mrs. Marion Gray,	Armagh,
	50	"	John Wallace,	Thos. R. Porter and another,	Ramsley,

SECOND STATUTORY TERM

DOWN.—*continued.*

Area of Holding Down	Poor Law Valuation	Rent of Holding prior to creation of First Statutory Term	Judicial Rent for First Statutory Term	Judicial Rent for Second Statutory Term	Observations.	Value of Tenancy.
A. R. P.	£ s. d.	£ s. d.	£ s. d.	£ s. d.		£ s. d.
9 0 15	1 9 0	9 15 0	5 5 0	6 0 0		
11 2 5	11 13 0	18 1 0	9 10 0	6 4 0		
6 0 10	8 6 0	7 10 0	6 0 0	6 6 0		
11 5 13	17 0 0	16 0 0	13 10 0	9 10 0		
84 1 0	25 8 0	39 15 0	23 10 0	16 15 0		
31 3 0	23 10 0	21 0 0	19 0 0	15 11 0		
6 0 31	8 15 0	9 1 8	7 12 8	5 15 0		
30 3 0	23 0 0	20 16 0	18 3 0	11 13 0		
34 0 0	16 8 0	23 17 6	18 10 0	19 0 0		
6 5 5	9 15 0	10 12 0	8 10 0	5 5 0		
6 0 10	13 15 0	10 0 0	5 4 0	5 0 0		
6 1 25	unascertained	11 0 0	6 10 0	6 15 0		
-19 3 37	11 7 6	18 13 6	18 0 0	6 15 0		
9 8 6	11 0 0	10 6 8	9 0 0	6 6 0		
16 1 20	15 7 6	21 8 6	17 10 0	11 10 0		
11 1 11	11 10 0	16 0 0	10 15 0	7 8 0		
11 1 16	9 6 0	13 0 0	11 0 0	7 0 0		
6 1 10	6 0 0	5 1 6	4 3 6	3 0 0		
37 3 0	17 0 0	19 15 3	16 1 0	10 11 6		
3 1 34	3 0 0	3 16 0	9 7 0	8 0 0		
6 9 15	6 16 0	7 15 10	6 2 0	4 7 8		
16 3 16	16 10 0	18 3 0	13 0 0	10 6 6		
6 0 0	7 10 0	7 5 0	5 6 8	3 15 0		
22 3 19	33 0 0	26 9 0	19 15 0	13 0 0		
43 0 30	84 10 0	32 15 3	30 6 0	24 0 0		
30 0 0	30 0 0	69 9 5	18 17 0	18 10 0		
37 0 0	35 0 0		23 17 6	16 0 0		
37 1 39	25 16 0	37 5 4	26 8 6	16 0 0		
2,977 3 18	2,940 6 0	3,354 16 11	2,859 6 4	1,947 19 10		

IRISH LAND COMMISSION.

SECOND STATUTORY TERM.

Name of Assistant Commissioner by whom Cases were decided.	Record Number.	Date of Order.	Name of Tenant.	Name of Landlord.	Townland.
Assistant Commissioners— A. R. Montgomery, A. S. Drane.	17	1887, Feb. 27,	Wm. G. Walsh, —	Rev. D. O'Leary and anor., Trustees of M. O'Jones, deceased.	Oakley & Lergh.
	44	„	Simon Scads, ...	do. — ...	Lergh, —
	45	„	Christopher Boyd, —	do.	Oakley & Lergh.
	39	„	James Cauthern, ...	Mrs. Margaret Flovet and others, Trustees of Will of G. Flovet, deceased.	Lergy, —
	28	„	John P. Thorton, —	Earl of Erne, ...	Gortgarran and another.
	75	„	John Lynch, ...	Dacre Hamilton, —	Drumarvoram.
	80	„	Patrick Maguire, ...	Colonel J. G. Irvine, —	Lergy, —
	108	„	Francis Horton, ...	George G. Flynn, ...	Mullybony, —
	74	„	Charles Smyth, ...	Dacre Hamilton, ...	Drumarvoram,
	78	„	Francis Quigley, —	do. ...	do. —
	72	„	John Smyth, —	do. —	do. —
	73	„	James Lynch, ...	do. ...	do. —
	51	„	John Callaghan, ...	H. F. Maguire, a minor, by Eliza Maguire and Edward Murphy.	Carvary, —
	66	„	Wm. Armstrong, ...	Robert Moore and others,	Mullaghtoppe and another.
	68	„	Anne Shannon, and Brosks.	Captain W. Collum, —	Drumbaughlin,
	60	„	John Credden, —	William H. Hoirs, —	Kilturk, —
	88	„	James Spence, —	Dr. William Hamilton, —	Rutnophing, —
	114	„	Catherine Maguire, ...	Colonel J. G. Irvine, —	Lergy (part of)
	70	„	Bridget Maguire, ...	do.	do. —
	92	„	Hugh M'Caffrey, junr.,	do. —	Drumgarran,
	98	„	John M'Gra, —	do. —	Rutnophing,
	86	„	Edward Wormley, —	John Armstrong and anor.,	Kilgreenlappe,
	84	„	Robert Watson, ...	do.	do. —
	62	„	Patrick Monaghan, —	John Armstrong and others,	Ramsvally, —
	81	„	Thomas M'Brien, —	do. —	do. —
	80	„	Christopher Gamble, —	do. ... —	do. —
	85	„	Catherine M'After, —	Reps. of P. Mimo and agmy.	Tanyleand, —
	84	„	Robert Gam, —	do. —	do. —
	79	„	Bernard Monaghan, ...	do. —	do. —
	73	„	Elizabeth Forrest, ...	do. —	do. —
	77	„	Henry Black, ...	Captain William Collum, —	M'Pixie —
	76	„	Patrick Flanagan, ...	do.	do. —
	82	„	Edmund Ramsey, —	Mrs. Marion Grey, ...	Walsier. —

Extent of Holding including Turbary.	Poor Law Valuation.	Rent of Holding prior to sanction of First Statutory Term.	Judicial Rent for First Statutory Term.	Judicial Rent for Second Statutory Term.	Observations.
a. r. p.	£ s. d.	£ s. d.	£ s. d.	£ s. d.	
14 0 0	13 5 0	16 18 3	13 7 4	5 15 0	
18 3 10	13 0 0	18 15 4	13 10 0	9 0 0	
43 3 10	31 10 0	43 18 10	31 18 0	34 8 4	
31 3 0	15 5 0	21 10 0	17 10 0	13 18 0	
30 0 30	31 10 0	28 4 4	23 11 0	16 9 0	
38 1 7	13 15 0	13 5 0	13 10 0	10 0 0	
88 3 30	13 5 0	17 4 0	16 0 0	10 3 0	
63 1 10	24 10 0	27 0 0	23 5 0	18 7 0	
87 3 80	16 5 0	21 15 4	16 0 0	13 0 0	
13 3 30	7 15 0	8 5 5	8 10 0	5 10 0	
13 3 10	6 9 0	8 3 3	7 10 0	6 0 0	
14 3 86	9 0 0	9 5 0	8 0 0	6 10 0	
37 1 80	10 5 0	23 6 0	15 0 0	10 3 0	
35 3 30	20 3 0	27 0 0	22 0 0	14 0 0	
13 0 0	9 5 0	13 13 0	10 0 0	7 0 0	
63 1 80	37 15 0	38 13 5	34 10 0	23 13 0	
34 0 0	18 10 0	26 10 0	17 18 0	11 17 0	
67 1 80	18 5 0	13 8 0	18 10 0	8 10 0	
10 1 30	13 10 0	16 13 0	15 0 0	6 6 0	
65 3 5	13 0 0	13 18 0	11 10 0	8 6 0	
18 1 38	11 10 0	16 0 0	18 10 0	9 15 0	
7 1 30	6 6 0	10 0 0	7 0 0	5 0 0	
6 3 10	4 0 0	5 0 0	5 10 0	3 15 0	
31 0 38	37 0 0	80 0 0	31 0 0	18 0 0	
30 3 0	16 0 0	23 0 0	15 0 0	11 5 0	
16 3 30	11 10 0	16 0 0	13 10 0	9 0 0	
8 3 35	5 15 0	9 5 0	7 0 0	5 15 0	
9 0 30	5 15 0	10 0 0	6 15 0	4 0 0	
10 1 10	7 10 0	11 4 5	8 15 5	5 0 0	
34 3 38	25 10 0	30 0 0	30 0 0	18 0 5	
36 0 38	32 10 0	36 10 0	22 10 0	18 5 0	
19 3 0	14 0 0	18 0 0	15 0 0	11 15 0	
36 0 80	30 0 0	24 13 0	30 0 0	18 10 0	

SECOND STATUTORY TERM.

Name of Assistant Commissioners by whom Cases were decided.	Record Number.	Date of Order.	Name of Tenant.	Name of Landlord.	Townland.
Assistant Commissioners—		1897.			
G. H. Tuckey (Legal). B. Johnston. G. M'Elliott.	141	Jan. 6,	Thomas Plunkett,	John Madden,	Derryadd,
	129	March 31,	Francis Duncan,	Colonel John G. Irvine,	Drummullagh
	153	„	John W. Kerr,	Luke F Knight,	Aughnacloy and …
	134	„	Mary M'Nulty,	Mrs. Marian Gray,	Farranacushog & …
	172	„	John Rennick,	do.	do.
	161	„	Edward Moore,	Col. M. Archdale & anor.,	Drumarbeg,
	162	„	Charles Boyce,	Governors of Vaughan's Charity Schools.	Fiddens and anr.
	140	„	William M'Crea,	Hugh Barton,	Lowry,
	200	„	Hiram Darley,	William Hamilton,	Reingbing,
	112	„	Patrick Gunn junior,	Earl of Enniskillen,	Cornatooan,
	163	„	Patrick M'Mann,	Captain Wm. Collum,	Garraghey,
	133	„	William Kerr & anor.,	do.	Corlogan,
	173	„	Catherine M'Nulty,	do.	Mackinagh,
	180	„	James Gormley, Admix. of Edward Gormley.	Colonel John G. Irvine,	Clamphigh,
G. H. Tuckey (Legal). A. R. Pratt. B. J. Cham.	133	March 22,	John Dougan,	John Armstrong & others,	Bommully,
	132	„	Mary Quigley,	do.	do.
	147	„	Cath. Keenan, Admix. of Bernard Keenan.	do.	do.
	213	„	Do.	do.	do.
	136	„	John Boyle,	do.	do.
	183	Jan. 15,	Dr. Alex. W. Flood,	Capt. A. H. M. H. Joyce,	Belcoo East and West.
	211	March 31,	Christopher Rochussen,	William H. Archdale,	Rossdhu,
	253	„	Hugh Feenan,	do.	Teal,
	160	„	William Scallan,	Captain A. H. Jones,	Cavanagarrigh and another.
	185	„	Patrick Timmony,	do.	Ederneelagh,
	173	„	Patrick Lilly,	do.	Carraghan,
	301	„	Denis Lilly,	do.	Monamurragh,
	108	„	Mary Murphy,	Earl of Enniskillen,	Crockaunarry,
	162	„	Robert Dane,	do.	Derryhillagh,
	204	„	Hugh Murphy,	do.	Clantiff,
	44	„	Owen Chevigan,	do.	Farthag,
	144	„	Peter Dolan,	do.	Kilmassi,
	315	„	John Magahan,	Mrs. A. G. Adams,	Artnagh,

SECOND STATUTORY TERM.

FERMANAGH—*continued.*

Extent of Holding Statute.	Poor Law Valuation.	Rent of Holding prior to agreement for First Statutory Term.	Judicial Rent for First Statutory Term.	Judicial Rent for Second Statutory Term.	Observations.	Value of Tenancy.
a. r. p.	£ s. d.	£ s. d.	£ s. d.	£ s. d.		£ s. d.
11 0 13	7 18 0	7 18 6	6 18 6	5 15 0	By consent.	
15 0 25	17 0 0	16 1 0	17 0 0	18 15 0		
18 1 16	15 10 0	23 5 6	18 0 0	21 17 10		
39 1 0	28 0 0	34 16 8	27 0 0	22 5 0		
15 1 23	18 0 0	13 15 10	14 10 0	12 0 0		
14 3 10	47 0 0	44 0 0	32 0 0	43 0 0		
23 3 5	31 5 0	24 7 0	19 0 0	18 10 0		
16 1 5	15 0 0	14 0 0	11 11 4	6 12 0		
14 1 0	14 3 0	23 0 0	13 0 0	18 10 0		
19 1 21	11 10 0	13 0 0	13 0 0	9 10 11		
51 3 10	34 0 0	27 0 0	40 3 1	38 10 0		
51 0 50	33 3 0	48 17 8	43 0 0	60 0 0		
19 0 10	20 10 0	23 10 0	24 0 0	18 5 0		
43 3 15	17 10 0	22 0 0	17 10 0	16 3 0		
10 1 56	7 15 0	11 10 0	8 0 0	5 3 0		
15 1 30	11 10 0	16 10 0	12 0 0	9 0 0		
18 3 31	9 15 0	14 4 0	11 0 0	7 17 0		
4 0 7	4 15 0	4 6 0	5 10 0	3 13 0		
17 1 10	13 0 0	17 0 0	13 0 0	9 4 0		
31 3 0	23 12 0	30 0 0	28 12 0	23 13 0	By consent.	
31 3 12	21 15 0	20 0 0	23 10 0	17 0 0		
22 1 5	13 10 0	15 0 0	11 0 0	8 0 0		
13 1 14	10 5 0	14 1 5	10 13 0	8 0 0		
44 0 0	29 13 0	26 0 3	27 0 0	21 0 0		
19 1 20	4 0 0	5 4 11	6 0 0	3 5 0		
61 1 0	6 15 0	12 3 7	5 0 0	6 13 0		
15 1 0	8 14 0	13 6 0	10 0 0	9 0 0		
15 0 30	27 10 0	25 0 0	25 0 0	20 0 0		
17 0 0	9 3 0	11 5 0	9 15 5	6 0 0		
77 3 25	13 5 0	17 0 0	15 0 0	12 0 0		
105 1 5	19 5 0	20 0 0	19 0 0	14 5 0		
17 3 35	15 0 0	19 5 0	16 10 0	10 0 0		

L

SECOND STATUTORY TERM.

COUNTY OF

Names of Assistant Commissioners by whom Cases were decided.	Record Number.	Date of Order.	Name of Tenant.	Name of Landlord.	Townland.
Assistant Commissioners—		1897.			
C. H. Toleken (Legal). A. S. Deane. E. J. Crane.	163	March 22,	John Patterson,	John A. Irwin,	Cartaghan,
	204	"	Jane Reilly,	do.	Scalingh,
	325	"	Anne M'Caffery,	Mrs. Marion Gray,	Scalingh,
	562	"	James Magovern,	Christopher L'Estrange,	Aughnmore,
	178	"	John Parker,	Mrs. Lizzie Fleming & ors.,	Drumard,
	175	"	Michael Gaffini,	do.	do.
	166	"	Patrick M'Murray,	London M. Nixon & others,	Lennan,
	188	"	Thomas Brownlee,	do.	do.
	164	"	Michael M'Loughlin,	do.	do.
	544	"	Margaret Martin otherwise M'Mann,	Mrs. Marion Gray.	Whilliam,
					Total,

COUNTY OF

Assistant Commissioners—	109	March 8,	Thomas H. Moore,	Mrs. Caroline H. Beresford,	Clondermot,
D. Torme (Legal). M. Spottle. J. M. Kelle.	187	"	Mrs. Eliza Michaels,	Captain O. L. Davidson,	Eglinton,
	129	"	Samuel Young,	Lord Templemore,	Coologrin,
	204	"	James O'Doherty,	do.	Whitehouse,
	301	"	John Harkin,	Rose S. M. de la P. Beresford,	Carnreagh,
	673	"	Justin Kartin,	do.	do.
	634	"	Frederick Ormsby,	do.	do.
	638	"	John Donaghy & anoth.,	do.	do.
	633	"	William Donaghy,	do.	do.
	392	"	John M'Callion,	George Kane,	Ballot,
	394	"	Edward Lynch,	do.	Proben,
	541	"	John Lynn,	do.	Dunloagh,
	64	"	James Crawford,	Hon. The Irish Society,	Ravenaghloaf,
	67	"	John Brown,	do.	do.
	180	"	William Orr,	do.	Sheriff Mountain,
	708	"	James O'Doherty,	do.	do.
	363	"	Mary Ann Gillespie,	George Kane,	Brick Kiln,

SECOND STATUTORY TERM

FERMANAGH—*continued.*

Extent of Holding. Statute.	Poor Law Valuation.	Rent of Holding prior to revision of first Statutory Term.	Judicial Rent for First Statutory Term.	Judicial Rent for Second Statutory Term.	Observations.	Value of Tenancy.
A. R. P.	£ s. d.	£ s. d.	£ s. d.	£ s. d.		£ s. d.
41 0 23	23 0 0	31 11 2	25 10 0	17 8 0		
4 1 25	7 0 0	9 12 8	7 10 0	5 1 0		
17 3 23	13 0 0	16 11 0	13 6 0	10 0 0		
77 3 10	7 10 0	18 0 0	16 10 0	10 17 0	And right of grazing over 397 a.	
34 3 34	19 0 0	24 8 8	18 10 0	14 7 0	1 a. 10r. adjoining mountain.	
18 1 38	14 8 0	13 8 0	12 0 0	9 0 0		
30 3 23	23 10 0	30 8 6	23 0 0	17 0 0		
47 0 23	33 10 0	41 13 6	36 0 0	27 15 8		
8 1 10	5 5 0	7 14 8	5 10 0	4 10 0		
18 2 16	12 8 0	16 19 0	14 0 0	10 15 0		
1,173 3 33	1,303 1 0	1,573 7 6½	1,377 6 5	843 4 3		

LONDONDERRY.

71 1 37	86 0 0	66 5 0	55 0 0	41 5 0		
38 1 0	63 0 0	60 0 0	56 0 0	34 6 0		
53 1 8	37 0 0	41 0 0	33 11 0	24 18 0		
63 3 34	39 0 0	86 0 0	25 10 0	13 10 0		
16 3 23	4 10 6	4 0 0	5 0 0	3 10 0		
35 0 10	9 15 0	11 0 0	5 16 0	4 16 0		
36 0 0	15 0 0	14 19 0	11 10 0	4 6 0		
33 2 23	6 5 0	10 11 0	6 0 0	5 15 0		
36 0 13	10 0 0	10 0 0	6 5 0	5 0 0		
13 3 34	16 5 0	13 0 0	10 10 0	9 7 0		
5 1 10	9 5 0	10 6 0	7 16 0	6 9 0		
34 1 18	34 10 0	33 10 0	27 5 0	21 0 5		
13 0 0	18 0 0	13 8 8	14 15 0	11 0 0		
41 1 0	30 10 0	31 0 0	9 15 0	8 0 0		
33 1 3	9 10 0	11 13 3	8 10 0	5 10 0		
41 0 0	31 0 0	37 4 6	29 0 0	80 0 0		
7 1 13	6 10 0	6 13 0	6 0 0	3 0 0		

SECOND STATUTORY TERM.

COUNTY OF

Names of Assistant Commissioners by whom Cases were decided.	Record Number	Date of Order.	Name of Tenant.	Name of Landlord.	Townland.
Assistant Commissioners :—		1897.			
J. MacKenzie, L. W. Byrne.	5	March 1,	James Anderson,	Mrs. Maria L. Rankin,	Ballymoney,
	13	"	John Doherty	Sir Henry H. Bruen, Bart.,	Dartrees,
	23	"	Kennedy Moore,	C. M. Gage & others, Reps. of Mrs. H. Scott,	Ballynacannon,
	20	"	William M'Neill,	Nathaniel Alexander,	Aghadowey,
	31	"	Matilda Glenn,	Thomas Montgomery,	Dunloanan,
	37	"	James M'Callum,	Colonel R. J. Harkins,	Islandmaskin,
	16	"	William Forbes,	James Boles,	Wardyhall,
	18	"	John Carry,	James Hannay,	Cornabay,
	15	"	James Harrison,	do.	do.
	23	"	Thomas Canning,	Mrs. Barbara Torrens and another,	Coalal,
	34	"	Michael Lynch,	do.	Tibarrea,
	15	"	James M'Clister,	do.	do.
	23	"	Bernard M'Kee,	do.	Killead,
	10	"	William Workman,	Edward Mullen,	Mananylennan,
	9	"	Alexander Miller,	do.	do.
	12	"	James Poden,	do.	do.
	11	"	William Workman,	do.	do.
	18	"	Matthew Brown,	Grace T. Hay and others,	East Crannagh,
					Total

COUNTY OF

Assistant Commissioners:—	124	March 27,	Thomas Ferguson,	Richard Nugent & another, Trees. of Thomas Hamilton,	Carrigahin,
J. H. Byrne (Legal), M. A. Patterson, J. B. R. Mowbray.	229	"	Francis Duffy,	do.	do.
	231	"	Patrick Conlan,	do.	do.
	228	"	Anne Duffy,	do.	do.
	230	"	Pat Duffy,	do.	Garryhorn,
	227	"	Peter Conlan (Stephen),	do.	do.
	115	"	James Fitzpatrick,	do.	do.
	124	"	John Walsh,	do.	do.
	223	"	Owen M'Guckian,	do.	Carrigahin,
	236	"	Eleanor Harkness, Wife of Robert Harkness,	R. G. Leslie,	Drunan,

SECOND STATUTORY TERM.

LONDONDERRY—*continued.*

Extent of Holding in Statute Acres.	Poor Law Valuation.	Rent of Holding prior to commission at Pre-Statutory Term.	Judicial Rent for First Statutory Term.	Judicial Rent for Second Statutory Term.	Observations.	Value of Tenancy.
A. R. P.	£ s. d.	£ s. d.	£ s. d.	£ s. d.		£ s. d.
20 1 8	23 0 0	26 0 8	21 5 0	19 0 0		
24 0 0	—	28 0 0	22 0 0	20 2 0		
14 1 0	24 10 0	24 16 1	16 0 0	11 5 0		
14 3 10	12 18 0	16 0 0	13 10 0	8 1 0		
64 1 25	70 18 0	110 0 0	73 0 0	43 5 5		
4 3 20	8 10 0	14 0 0	8 0 0	7 3 0		
74 1 23	34 10 0	44 14 0	33 0 0	25 16 0		
34 1 0	25 5 0	37 18 3	27 0 0	23 16 5		
1 1 33	unascertained	10 4 11	7 0 0	6 10 0		
20 0 0	9 10 0	11 1 6	6 10 0	4 7 0		
44 6 14	8 0 0	11 1 6	6 15 0	6 15 0		
44 0 0	8 3 0	13 12 0	8 15 0	7 17 0		
144 0 14	73 15 0	38 4 3	26 0 0	21 1 0		
64 3 25	59 10 0	84 0 0	52 0 0	43 17 5		
18 1 21	14 0 0	16 11 4	18 10 0	9 5 0		
23 4 7	14 5 0	19 17 1	13 0 0	11 3 0		
4 4 23	2 3 0	0 11 4	3 10 0	2 5 0		
3 1 0	4 14 0	6 10 0	5 0 0	3 13 0		
1,123 3 20	649 18 0	835 10 7	705 0 0	543 4 5		

MONAGHAN.

13 1 25	7 0 0	8 16 0	6 12 6	6 12 5		
20 1 0	18 5 0	17 5 6	13 5 0	6 13 0		
17 3 15	13 15 0	15 16 0	18 10 0	8 11 2		
28 0 31	25 0 0	30 5 10	23 0 0	16 0 2		
22 2 10	15 5 0	21 1 5	17 7 6	12 16 3		
10 1 15	8 0 0	10 19 4	7 16 0	5 0 5		
7 9 20	5 15 0	7 15 6	6 17 6	4 8 3		
19 1 20	16 0 0	16 0 0	14 13 6	10 16 5		
21 3 20	17 10 0	21 17 3	16 0 0	12 1 5		
31 1 25	unascertained	26 18 5	21 5 0	16 16 11		

IRISH LAND COMMISSION.

SECOND STATUTORY TERM

COUNTY OF

Names of Assistant Commissioners by whom Cases were decided.	Record Number.	Date of Order.	Name of Tenant.	Name of Landlord.		Townland.	
Assistant Commissioners—		1887.					
J. H. Kent (Legal). M. S. Patterson. J. G. S. Mowbray.	796	March 27,	Robert Mills,	R. G. Leslie,	...	Drumgrole,	
	801	"	Thomas Potor,	do.		Drumgrole others,	and
	796	"	Matilda Mills,	do.		Drumgrole another,	and
	797	"	Henry Gilbert,	do.		Cortroman,	
	300	"	James Stout,	do.		do.	
	197	"	John Ellis,	O'B. Cole,		Crieve,	
	192	"	James Keenan,	do.		do.	
	199	"	Patrick Smyth,	do.		do.	
	200	"	Francis M'Cahoy	do.		do.	
	290	"	George Scott,	Lord Rope and others,		Drumgrole Lr.,	
M. F. Crean (Legal). J. D. Boyd. L. Creen.	122	Feb. 25,	Archibald Harper,	R. C. B. Chaddeston,		Cortabber,	
	173	"	Joseph Duffy,	Thomas Goote and another,		Carolina,	
	119	"	Patrick Nolan, Ltd. Admor. of Peter Nolan, deceased.	do.		Aghaboy,	
	118	"	Patrick M'Keown,	do.		Crove,	
	120	"	John M'Keown,	do.		Cortell,	
	110	"	Michael Cassah,	do.		do.	
	115	"	James Fitzpatrick,	do.		do.	
	316	"	Mary Donoghue,	do.		do.	
	108	"	John M'Dermott,	do.		do.	
	116	"	James Kernaghan,	do.		Fingh,	
	131	"	Miss M'Phillips,	do.		do.	
	110	"	James Clarke,	do.		do.	
	108	"	Edwd. M'Mahon, Ltd. Admor. of Edward M'Mahon, deceased.	do.		do.	
	137	"	Hugh Duffy,	do.		Carolina,	
	114	"	John Smyth,	do.		do.	
	107	"	James Clarke,	do.		do.	
J. H. Kent (Legal). G. J. G. Adamson. W. Jewson.	172	March 9,	Barter M'Mahon,	Lord Rossmore,	...	Nobbkirk and another,	
	196	"	James Corbley,	Edward J. Lacon,	...	Derrypillory,	
	301	"	William Brown,	Henry Crawford,	...	Cormwave,	

SECOND STATUTORY TERM.

MONAGHAN—continued.

Area of Holding.	Poor Law Valuation.	Rent of Holding prior to revision of First Statutory Term.	Judicial Rent for First Statutory Term.	Judicial Rent for Second Statutory Term.	Observations.	Value of Tenancy.
A. R. P.	£ s. d.	£ s. d.	£ s. d.	£ s. d.		£ s. d.
17 2 23		23 11 6	19 0 0	15 5 4		
19 1 20	17 0 0	18 18 10	18 11 5	10 6 7		
20 2 35	15 10 0	19 8 6	16 11 0	14 1 10		
9 2 30	14 15 0	15 5 6	10 10 0	5 3 8		
18 3 30	17 10 0	21 7 2	15 7 6	11 3 11		
13 0 15	8 0 0	7 14 4	6 10 0	8 0 0		
20 1 30	13 15 0	19 19 3	19 10 3	15 19 9		
17 3 5	18 10 0	16 5 3	15 0 0	11 15 7		
20 0 10	21 5 0	21 15 8	8 10 0	7 7 7		
20 0 23	55 8 0	55 0 0	57 0 0	33 7 0		
20 0 20	17 10 0	23 9 8	16 10 0	15 18 6		
17 1 0	13 0 0	17 13 8	13 0 0	8 9 0		
24 3 0	20 10 0	25 15 10	21 0 0	18 5 0		
7 8 0	8 0 0	10 8 10	6 10 0	5 10 0		
24 1 20	16 10 0	27 17 0	17 10 0	15 0 0		
16 7 37	13 0 0	17 15 4	13 10 0	11 5 0		
23 1 20	16 10 0	25 15 5	21 0 0	14 16 0		
43 3 0	32 0 0	46 2 10	34 0 0	28 0 0		
11 0 15	13 5 0	15 15 8	15 0 0	10 10 0		
11 0 20	7 15 0	9 1 3	5 0 0	4 3 0		
17 0 25	21 0 0	21 1 0	20 10 0	14 0 6		
18 3 10	13 10 8	14 13 0	12 10 8	8 17 0		
25 2 6	19 5 0	23 5 0	18 0 0	14 8 0		
9 0 20	6 15 0	6 10 0	7 10 0	5 0 0		
13 3 9	10 0 0	15 15 0	10 0 0	8 15 0		
13 9 22	10 0 0	12 8 8	10 0 0	6 17 0		
29 1 5	19 15 0	21 19 11	19 5 0	13 5 0		
28 0 25	26 0 0	29 1 10	24 0 0	11 3 0		
5 5 20	9 10 0	3 15 0	3 3 0	1 6 0		

SECOND STATUTORY TERM.

Names of Assistant Commissioners by whom Cases were decided	Record Number	Date of Cases	Name of Tenant	Name of Landlord	Townland
Assistant Commissioners—		1891.			
J. R. Edge (Legal). G. A. C. Anderson. W. Jephson.	307	March 9,	Alexander Wallace,	Edward S. Lowe,	Grove South,
	339	„	John Balleagh,	do.	Llangeeny,
	149	„	James Moffatt,	do.	Avellum,
	160	„	Do.,	do.	Grove South,
	324	„	Francis M'Guire,	Miss Anne Marie Gorman and another,	Avileragh,
	234	„	Mary Ronaghan, Ltd. Admix. of Patrick Ronaghan, deceased.	do.	do.
	163	„	Michael M'Kenny,	do.	do.
	191	„	William Tate,	do.	do.
	176	„	Eliza Lentham,	do.	do.
	173	„	Edward Curraghan,	do.	do.
	310	„	Hugh Barker, Ltd. Admr. of Bridget Barker, deceased.	Edward J. Richardson,	Craighan,
	154	„	Henry Lowry,	do.	Thinwers and another,
	177	„	John Farrell,	Henry Crawford,	Cordanlough,
	173	„	Hugh Lenny,	do.	Cordanlough and another,
	157	March 22,	Sarah Cooper,	Lord Plunkett,	Dangory,
	369	„	Robert Pringle,	James J. Wright and another,	Ballinahone,
	303	„	William Hadley,	Nathaniel Cooke,	Clonwaven,
	251	„	James Ward,	S. K. Twigg,	Carntamurg,
	243	„	Peter M'Kievlan,	Rev. Samuel Atkinson,	Corraguill,
	370	„	Peter Callaghan,	Sir Robert Ferster,	Derrynamagh,
	253	„	Anne Maguire, Ltd. Admix. of Peter Maguire, deceased.	do.	do.
	316	„	Terence M'Closkey,	do.	do.
	402	„	Patrick Mears,	John M'Birney,	Carontore,
	201	„	James Mears,	do.	do.
	69	„	James Smith,	do.	do.
	205	„	Mary J. Clarke, Ltd. Admix. of James Clarke.	Francis K. Jones and others,	Cardalough,
	422	„	William M'Birney,	do.	do.
	174	„	Francis M'Garry,	Thomas Clarke and another,	Grove,
					Total

SECOND STATUTORY TERM

MONAGHAN—*continued.*

Extent of Holding, Statute.	Poor Law Valuation.	Rent of Holding prior to creation of First Statutory Term.	Judicial Rent for First Statutory Term.	Judicial Rent for Second Statutory Term.	Observations.	Value of Tenancy.
A. R. P.	£ s. d.	£ s. d.	£ s. d.	£ s. d.		£ s. d.
19 1 4	14 15 0	19 7 4	16 0 0	9 3 0		
10 1 4	8 5 0	8 17 10	7 0 0	5 10 0		
61 2 25	37 5 0	43 0 0	35 0 0	23 10 0		
71 0 37	59 8 0	78 1 4	60 0 0	36 0 0		
5 2 10	8 8 0	8 0 0	5 15 0	3 16 0		
5 1 65	6 0 0	7 3 3	4 0 0	3 15 0		
4 0 30	4 0 0	5 5 4	4 0 0	2 7 0		
3 1 4	1 10 0	8 4 4	1 7 6	0 15 0		
16 0 0	6 0 0	12 6 8	10 0 0	4 17 0		
13 2 4	3 15 0	14 0 0	11 0 0	4 5 0		
36 0 15	34 10 0	30 2 0	23 5 0	15 10 0		
23 0 15	14 5 0	23 5 0	21 15 0	13 5 0		
18 0 20	10 15 0	13 1 0	9 3 0	5 14 0		
11 0 55	6 8 0	10 15 0	6 15 0	5 13 0		
1 3 18	2 15 0	8 10 0	3 10 0	1 10 0		
138 2 5	150 10 0	123 0 0	93 0 0	74 0 0		
38 0 0	33 0 0	36 5 3	19 10 0	16 3 0		
8 1 0	7 10 0	6 13 3	7 0 0	4 0 0		
17 1 17	5 10 0	6 1 0	5 10 0	3 6 0		
19 1 4	3 0 0	5 4 5	4 5 0	3 2 0		
15 0 35	8 0 0	4 16 4	4 5 0	3 10 0		
20 2 51	7 0 0	6 8 0	5 10 0	4 16 0		
4 3 8	4 0 0	3 13 0	4 15 5	2 5 0		
5 2 0	3 10 0	1 8 2	5 17 8	1 16 0		
5 1 39	6 10 0	4 7 5	3 10 11	4 15 0		

SECOND STATUTORY TERM.

Names of Assistant Commissioners by whom Cases were decided.	Record Number.	Date of Order.	Name of Tenant.	Name of Landlord.	Townland.
Assistant Commissioners—		1897.			
J. H. Rowe (Legal). J. Howlin. W. Small.	304	March 3,	Robert J. Johnston,	Averill Lloyd, —	Tamnymore,
	333	"	Patrick M'Cormack, Ltd. Admor. of Mary M'Cormack,	do.	do.
	254	Feb. 17,	Andrew Stewart,	John H. O'Neill,	Ranaghan,
	412	"	Ellen Hamil,	Major William Chaine,	Mullaghboy,
	152	"	Richard Redd,	do.	do.
	155	"	John Farley,	do.	Bramley & ano,
	130	"	Jane Harvey, Ltd. Admor. of Hugh Harvey,	Mrs. Maria Harris,	Garvagh,
	173	"	Neal M'Gurk,	Mrs. Elizabeth Irwin,	Mullyrattan,
	134	"	Gerard Stewart, Ltd. Admor. of George Redd,	Major Robert J. Howard,	Annaghmore,
	213	"	William Murroe,	do.	Overagh Lower,
	925	"	James M'Kenzie,	Mrs. Jane C. Clarke,	Drumlea,
	394	"	Do.,	do.	do.
	211	"	John M'Kenzie,	do.	Drumbeg,
	210	"	Thomas M'Kenzie,	do.	do.
	908	"	John Lappin,	do.	Tullylure,
	906	"	Neil Cassidy,	do.	Mangrmore,
	687	"	John Kerr,	Rev. Alexander S. Irwin,	Banting & ano,
	148	"	John M'Gurk,	do.	do.
	149	"	John Heatherington,	do.	do.
	138	"	Maurice Quinn,	do.	do.
	421	"	Margaret Ward,	do.	do.
	147	"	John Heatherington,	do.	do.
	144	"	John Raffery,	do.	Derryinbrook,
	145	"	Arthur Mallon,	do.	do.
	141	"	Daniel Hughes,	do.	do.
	139	"	Hugh Ardern,	do.	do.
	139	"	Patrick Arthurs,	do.	do.
	135	"	Daniel Waggin,	do.	do.
	146	"	Denis M'Gurk,	do.	do.
	336	"	James Mallon and another,	do.	Kildynamboy,
	342	"	Henry M'Curry,	do.	do.
	854	"	Charles Donnelly,	do.	do.
	945	"	Do.,	do.	do.

SECOND STATUTORY TERM.

TYRONE.

Extent of Holding Statute Acres.	Poor Law Valuation.	Rent of Holding prior to creation of Present Statutory Term.	Judicial Rent for First Statutory Term.	Judicial Rent for Second Statutory Term.	Observations.	Value of Tenancy.
A. R. P.	£ s. d.	£ s. d.	£ s. d.	£ s. d.		£ s. d.
7 0 0	5 5 0	8 17 8	4 18 0	3 15 9		
4 3 0	7 10 0	10 0 0	7 15 0	5 10 0		
9 0 0	10 15 0	15 0 0	10 10 0	7 5 10		
8 0 7	5 10 0	6 10 0	8 0 0	5 14 8		
13 5 0	14 10 0	15 15 0	18 15 0	10 1 9		
10 0 0	5 5 0	10 2 0	7 10 0	5 5 7		
5 0 0	Uncertained.	5 0 0	4 10 0	3 17 0		
7 0 3	6 5 0	7 15 0	5 15 0	4 4 5		
13 3 13	14 10 0	17 11 0	13 10 0	8 3 9		
11 1 8	23 15 0	24 13 0	23 0 0	15 4 4		
9 3 20	10 5 0	13 0 0	10 0 0	5 11 8		
5 3 30	5 15 0	8 10 0	4 8 0	1 17 8		
13 0 5	43 0 0	50 0 0	40 0 0	36 14 2		
35 3 20	43 10 0	50 0 0	40 0 0	17 9 11		
21 1 7	22 10 0	30 0 0	34 0 0	14 17 4		
11 3 17	18 0 0	20 0 0	15 6 0	9 19 6		
13 3 8	10 5 0	17 3 9	10 0 0	5 15 1		
5 1 20	5 10 0	9 17 1	7 5 9	4 15 8		
15 3 3	11 15 0	18 0 0	13 10 9	3 18 7		
63 3 25	57 10 0	63 5 0	54 10 0	15 10 9		
9 0 5	Uncertained.	30 0 0	7 5 0	5 13 1		
6 1 0	do.	14 15 3	5 5 0	5 17 3		
5 0 15	7 10 0	10 11 3	6 15 0	5 8 8		
57 1 13	16 5 9	18 5 5	15 15 0	9 16 3		
16 0 9	15 5 0	21 7 4	16 0 0	10 5 8		
6 3 5	7 0 0	8 0 0	5 0 0	4 9 9		
6 0 35	5 0 5	7 4 0	4 12 6	5 6 1		
23 0 83	11 5 0	16 15 5	13 0 0	5 15 5		
7 0 35	8 15 0	11 4 4	6 10 0	4 15 5		
15 1 63	13 10 0	19 0 0	16 5 0	9 6 5		
5 3 8	5 5 0	5 17 0	5 0 0	2 3 2		
13 1 16	10 0 0	16 17 2	9 15 0	7 5 1		
15 1 80	6 5 0	14 19 5	9 10 0	7 15 5		

SECOND STATUTORY TERM.

Names of Acting Organisations by whom Cases were Settled.	Record Number.	Date of Order.	Name of Tenant.	Name of Landlord.	Townland.
Aberdeen Companies &c.—		1897.			
J. R. Bruce (Legal). J. Howlin. W. Small.	153	Feb. 27.	Edward Madden,	Rev. Alexander S. Irwin,	Killybrackey,
	124	„	Patrick Riordan,	do.	do.
	154	„	John Donaghy,	do.	do.
	153	„	Hugh O'Donnell,	do.	Ramlog,
G. H. Tarleton (Legal). E. Johnston. G. M'Elhatto.	216	March 15.	Hugh M'Grade,	Col. John D. Johnston,	Clonallagh,
	163	„	Patrick Kerr,	do.	Drumbarry,
	56	„	Joseph M'Laughlin,	do.	Balloghgourn,
G. N. Caldwell. J. Howlin.	43	March 5.	Alexander Foster,	Samuel Johnston,	Anybrind,
	31	„	Jas. M'Aleer, Ldd. Admor. of Peter M'Aleer.	Elizabeth J. M'Causland and others.	Drumnahilly,
	39	„	John Carvey,	do.	do.
	32	„	John Daly (Townley),	do.	do.
	16	„	Do.	do.	do.
	35	„	Patrick Kerr,	do.	do.
	35	„	John Daly (Larry),	do.	do.
	33	„	John Daly (Hugh),	do.	do.
	30	„	Charles Kerr,	do.	do.
	61	„	Hannah M'Crory, Ldd. Administratrix of Pat M'Crory, deceased.	do.	Killygeowagh and another.
	53	„	John M'Aleer,	do.	Drumnahilly,
	37	„	Michael Carvey,	do.	do.
	38	„	John Daly (Felix),	do.	do.
	39	„	Owen M'Aleer,	do.	do.
	35	„	Margaret Badforty,	do.	Fanagh,
	36	„	Patrick Treany,	do.	Fantry,
	93	„	Edward Treany,	do.	do.
	57	„	James M'Aleer,	do.	Drumnahilly,
	61	„	David Crawford,	Rev. P. Hackett, C.C.,	Gartnaham,
	62	„	Michael Hannigan,	W. S. Curry, a minor, by Charlotte Curry, his mother and next friend.	Oxby,
	64	„	Patrick Treany,	Catherine Cush,	Donaewry,
	70	„	William Porter,	Edward D. Martin,	Rough and others.

SECOND STATUTORY TERM.

TYRONE—*continued.*

Amount of Holding.	Poor Law Valuation.	Rent of Holding prior to coming of First Statutory Term.	Judicial Rent for First Statutory Term.	Judicial Rent for Second Statutory Term.	Observations.	Value of Tenancy.
A. R. P.	£ s. d.	£ s. d.	£ s. d.	£ s. d.		£ s. d.
0 2 10	11 5 0	14 0 5	14 14 0	5 10 0		
0 3 16	10 10 0	16 0 0	11 10 0	7 10 0		
1 3 34	7 5 0	8 6 10	8 10 0	4 7 6		
0 3 27	7 15 0	13 10 0	6 18 0	6 6 0		
21 0 30	72 0 0	87 10 3	80 0 0	16 5 0		
20 1 7	20 0 0	23 5 0	16 0 0	15 17 0		
16 3 0	15 5 0	18 0 0	14 0 0	11 13 0		
5 0 0	5 0 0	6 0 0	6 0 0	3 5 0		
13 0 16	10 15 0	15 10 0	11 0 0	8 3 0		
14 1 30	9 5 0	14 12 0	8 0 0	6 12 0		
16 1 34	18 10 0	19 0 0	13 0 0	9 15 0		
28 1 10	9 10 0	11 0 0	8 0 0	5 6 0		
60 0 17	72 10 0	29 6 0	27 10 0	18 0 0		
46 1 30	10 10 0	15 14 0	20 0 0	8 0 0		
79 1 80	11 0 0	14 14 0	9 10 0	7 4 0		
52 1 16	10 0 0	12 12 0	9 5 0	7 4 0		
30 0 13	10 10 0	13 13 0	5 10 0	6 17 6		
36 3 32	18 10 0	22 14 0	18 10 0	16 10 0		
17 0 16	9 10 0	19 4 0	5 0 0	8 13 0		
13 0 27	6 13 0	8 13 0	4 10 0	3 3 5		
16 1 0	5 0 0	8 0 0	5 5 0	6 0 0		
42 0 0	17 0 0	21 0 0	16 0 0	11 3 0		
64 3 20	18 0 0	21 0 0	16 0 0	13 10 0		
14 3 0	8 5 0	15 0 0	8 10 0	8 7 0		
13 3 11	9 10 0	16 0 0	9 0 0	7 7 0		
27 0 5	17 10 0	34 3 0	17 10 0	13 6 0		
13 4 37	13 8 0	15 15 0	13 10 0	9 8 0		
10 3 0	11 0 0	12 0 0	9 0 0	7 15 0		
47 8 10	37 10 0	61 0 0	35 0 5	27 10 0		

SECOND STATUTORY TERM.

COUNTY OF

Names of Assistant Commissioners by whom Cases were decided.	Record Number.	Date of Order.	Name of Tenant.	Name of Landlord.	Townland.
Assistant Commissioners—		1877.			
G. N. CALDWELL. J. HAWICK.	71	March 5,	William M'Cay, ...	The Misses Kelly, ...	Edergole Lane,
	72	"	Andrew Hutchinson,	Col. William Claims, ...	Gains,
	19	"	Edward M'Nulty, ...	J. Howard Dumley, ...	Kunshaberg,
	40	"	Thomas Watson, ...	Henry H. Stewart, ...	Gavin,
	80	"	William Dugan, ...	do., ...	Tullydarogh,
	70	"	Patrick M'Cormack, Admor. of Andrew M'Cormack, deceased	Maggie Smith ...	Drummanin,
	79	"	Robert J. Dugan, ...	Gardise Douglas and others, Trustees of Chaonie W. L. O'Kiley, deceased.	Linnadin,
	104	"	James M'Korhan, ...	do. ...	do.
	72	"	John Love, ...	do. ...	Rahonoy,
	89	"	George Armstrong ...	do. ...	do.
	84	"	Matthew Guy, ...	do. ...	do.
	85	"	John Hamilton, ...	do. ...	do.
	38	"	Thomas J. O'Brien, ...	do. ...	Tullynaliegh,
	68	"	Alexander M'Kinney,	do. ...	Tappen,
	19	"	Amos Guy, ...	do. ...	do.
	63	"	William Guy, senr., ...	do. ...	do.
	43	"	Do., ...	do. ...	Cartunnamilla,
	87	"	Jas. M'Kinney, junr.,	do. ...	do.
	29	"	Margaret Guy, ...	do. ...	do.
	16	"	Joseph Guy, ...	do. ...	do.
	18	"	William Smith, ...	do. ...	do.
	17	"	Do., ...	do. ...	Tullyver.
	83	"	Catherine M'Koom,	F. A. M. Moore,	Remilt.
	41	"	Francis M'Packard, ...	Lieut.-Gen. A. G. M. Moore,	Grange,
	75	"	James Mayers, ...	Colonel J. Birney,	Tullamvort,
	76	"	Owen Connolly,	Dr. J. Sherry, ...	Ballyrebellan,
	87	"	Annie M'Aleon,	James H. Ramsey,	Mullaghkinney,
	89	"	Thomas Daly, ...	Miss Jane Nulty,	Kanahberk,
	18	"	Mary M'Keown, ...	do. ...	Clarmell,
	61	"	Peter Guy, ...	do. ...	do.
	80	"	John M'Anally, ...	do. ...	do.

SECOND STATUTORY TERM.

TYRONE—continued.

Extent of Holding Quantity	Poor Law Valuation	Rent of Holding prior to stopping Former Statutory Term	Judicial Rent for First Statutory Term	Judicial Rent for Second Statutory Term	Observations	Value of Tenancy
A. R. P.	£ s. d.	£ s. d.	£ s. d.	£ s. d.		£ s. d.
11 3 5	7 10 0	5 10 0	7 5 0	5 15 0		
23 2 10	31 5 0	14 10 0	13 0 0	9 0 0		
13 0 4	7 0 0	10 15 0	6 10 0	5 0 0		
20 1 7	13 0 0	18 10 0	11 10 0	8 12 0		
50 1 0	27 0 0	17 0 0	20 0 0	17 5 0		
17 0 0	9 0 0	10 10 0	10 15 0	7 5 0		
34 0 7	17 10 0	20 0 5	15 10 0	13 5 0		
81 1 18	40 5 0	31 15 5	37 0 0	35 15 0		
60 3 25	47 0 0	50 12 1	44 0 0	39 0 0		
43 1 83	34 5 0	25 0 0	23 0 0	16 15 0		
54 1 0	36 5 0	46 5 0	31 10 0	30 3 0		
43 3 50	47 0 0	45 15 4	40 0 0	30 10 0		
100 1 11	18 15 4	20 0 0	14 10 0	10 14 0		
60 3 23	43 10 0	64 11 3	41 10 0	28 0 0		
51 0 0	21 10 0	25 17 5	19 0 0	13 15 0		
16 0 75	11 5 0	14 5 0	14 0 0	13 15 0		
16 3 0	15 10 0	20 1 3	14 10 0	12 5 0		
6 0 0	23 5 0	20 19 3	23 0 0	21 5 0		
20 0 0	20 10 0	33 15 0	22 20 0	17 10 0		
16 1 15	30 0 0	23 1 0	24 5 0	27 17 5		
10 0 10	39 10 0	34 17 10	27 20 0	16 12 4		
15 2 0	14 10 0	14 10 7	14 10 0	11 7 4		
44 0 50	44 10 0	64 0 0	45 0 0	35 15 0		
20 0 0	11 10 0	20 10 0	19 10 0	15 10 0		
20 1 15	25 15 4	28 10 0	23 0 0	15 0 0		
75 1 16	14 10 0	23 0 0	18 10 0	11 12 0		
15 1 90	16 15 0	27 0 0	17 10 0	14 5 0		
20 1 23	8 10 0	8 15 0	6 5 0	6 15 0		
12 2 5	4 5 0	6 0 0	5 0 0	4 1 0		
15 1 10	7 10 0	13 10 0	8 5 0	5 3 0		
50 2 0	6 15 0	13 10 0	7 10 0	5 5 0		

SECOND STATUTORY TERM.

Name of Assistant Commissioners by whom Case was decided.	Record Number.	Date of Order.	Name of Tenant.	Name of Landlord.	Townland.
Assistant Commissioners—		1897.			
C. H. TERLINS (Legal). W. S. HUNT.	345	March 30,	John Waly, —	John Hughey, —	Ardarew,
	203	„	George Devine, ...	J. T. Russell, —	Kilkeagh,
	202	„	Do. —	do. ...	do.
	83	„	Hugh Doherty, ...	Hon. R. G. L. Cochrane and others,	New Row,
	446	„	Patrick Loughrey, ...	John Hughey, ...	Ardarew,
	254	„	John McCormack, —	Mrs. Jane Auchinleck, ...	Deniers,
	181	„	Peter Cunddy, Ltd. Admr. of Patrick Unuudy,	Audley & T. J. Leary and another, Reps. of Audley Caldwell,	Mannerpugh,
	877	„	Samuel McKeown, —	Audley & T. J. Leary and others.	do.
	316	„	William Crawford, ...	do. ...	do.
	226	„	Jane McCurren, Ltd. Admrl. of John McCurren.	do. ...	do.
	360	„	Jacob Gatlen, —	do. ...	Coolenberts,
	216	„	Robert McKeown, —	do. ...	Mannerpugh,
	257	„	James Webben, —	do. ...	Coolenberts,
	168	„	James Alexander, ...	Audley & T. J. Leary and another, Reps. of Audley Caldwell	Mannerpugh,
	187	„	William McCurren, ...	do. ...	do.
	185	„	John Cunddy, ...	do. ...	do.
	193	„	Alexander McCurren,	do. ...	do.
	192	„	William Oliver, —	do. ...	do.
	190	„	James Logue, —	do. ...	do.
					Total, —

PROVINCE OF

Name of Assistant Commissioners—		Date of Order.	Name of Tenant.	Name of Landlord.	Townland.
L. DAVIS (Legal). A. H. CURRY. G. S. SOMMER.	8	March 30,	James Fagan, —	Thomas Keene, ...	Aringoth,
	9	„	Andrew Durham, ...	The Right Hon. Hon. T. Hamilton,	Milverton, —
	10	„	Do. —	do. ...	Turnparks, —
	11	„	Do. —	do. ...	Shenicks Island,
	12	„	Do. —	do. ...	Turnparks, —
	13	„	Do. ...	do. ...	do.

SECOND STATUTORY TERM.

TYRONE—continued.

Extent of Holding. Statute.	Poor Law Valuation.	Rent of Holding prior to coming of First Statutory Term.	Judicial Rent for First Statutory Term.	Judicial Rent for Second Statutory Term.	Observations.	Value of Tenancy.
A. R. P.	£ s. d.	£ s. d.	£ s. d.	£ s. d.		£ s. d.
47 2 0	19 0 0	17 0 0	14 0 0	11 0 0		
14 2 0	11 0 0	14 12 0	12 5 0	9 11 0		
16 2 0	11 0 0	14 2 0	11 10 0	10 0 0		
46 0 0	80 0 0	46 15 0	36 0 0	24 10 0		
17 3 0	4 15 0	5 17 4	4 5 0	3 0 0		
87 1 38	11 0 0	14 10 0	11 0 0	9 0 0		
32 2 14	6 10 0	12 12 0	8 0 0	6 0 0		
61 0 0	5 0 0	8 10 0	5 10 0	4 5 0		
11 1 6	4 0 0	8 0 0	4 15 0	2 12 6		
18 3 5	8 0 0	4 0 0	2 0 0	1 10 0		
10 3 87	11 5 0	14 0 0	10 10 0	10 0 0		
10 3 20	8 15 0	8 10 0	6 10 0	4 5 0		
16 2 20	11 10 0	14 5 0	11 0 0	9 0 0		
13 0 5	3 5 0	4 16 0	3 10 0	5 0 0		
4 1 34	3 10 0	6 0 0	3 10 0	3 10 0		
44 0 20	14 10 0	21 3 0	13 10 0	9 15 0		
8 3 6	8 15 0	4 10 0	3 10 0	9 15 0		
16 3 20	8 5 0	7 10 0	5 5 0	4 13 0		
18 2 16	11 0 0	12 10 5	12 10 5	4 13 0		
1,583 2 21	1,614 15 4	2,122 0 4	1,454 15 0	1,125 0 4		

LEINSTER.

DUBLIN.

19 0 0	30 0 0	42 0 0	60 0 0	47 0 0	
9 2 33	8 5 0	18 18 2	14 0 0	16 10 0	
5 0 0	11 15 0	14 11 4	18 0 0	11 0 0	
11 0 0	6 15 0	12 0 0	22 0 0	13 0 0	
9 2 10	4 0 0	4 17 6	5 0 0	5 0 0	
26 1 20	29 15 0	61 19 1	46 0 0	35 10 0	

Names of Assistant Commissioners by whom Cases were decided.	Record Number	Date of Order	Name of Tenant.	Name of Landlord.	Townland.
Assistant Commissioners—		1887.			
L. Doyle (Legal). A. N. Carty. O. S. Bolster.	18	March 30,	Andrew Durban,	The Right Hon. Ion T. Hamilton.	Balnymichk
	16	„	Do.,	do.	do.
	17	„	Do.,	do.	St. Patrick's Island. Total.

Assistant Commissioners—	48	Feb. 28,	Thomas Rourke,	Lord Annaly,	Limpah,
M. T. Cahan (Legal). J. D. Boyd. L. Crawley.	43	„	John Donovan,	do.	Llewellanh,
	46	„	Owen M'Cormack,	Henry B. Armstrong,	Barra Mountain
	34	„	Christopher Barter,	Edward M. O'Ferrall,	Kilmainmore,
	63	„	Patrick Cox,	do.	do.
	31	„	Michael Powell,	Lord Gough,	Cloderia,
	29	„	Patrick Powell,	do.	do.
	28	„	Anne Doyer,	do.	Tacan,
	30	„	James M'Garry,	do.	Tullabatagah
	27	„	Thomas Lennard,	do.	do.
	26	„	Pat Mann,	do.	do.
	25	„	Bryan Quigley,	do.	do.
	10	„	Denis Quinn,	Thomas L. Lefroy,	Killaybegs,
	48	„	Arthur Quinn,	do.	do.
	14	„	Michael Duignan,	do.	do.
	45	„	Do.,	do.	Drumm,
	39	„	William Scanlon,	do.	do.
	42	„	James Kelly,	Col. W. H. King-Harman,	Lagan,
	47	„	Alice Mulvey,	do.	Ardanda,
	41	„	William Donnellon,	do.	Easl,
	40	„	Mary Coleman,	do.	do.
	36	„	Patrick Gill,	do.	do.
	35	„	Ellen Conner,	do.	do.
	37	„	Ellen Conyney,	do.	do.
	38	„	Bryan Hany,	do.	do.
					Total.

DUBLIN—*continued.*

Tenure of Holding. Baronies.	Poor Law Valuation.	Rent of Holding prior to reaction of First Statutory Term.	Judicial Rent for First Statutory Term.	Judicial Rent for Second Statutory Term.	Observations.	Value of Tenancy.
A. R. P.	£ s. d.	£ s. d.	£ s. d.	£ s. d.		£ s. d.
53 0 34	35 10 0	104 1 5	33 0 0	63 10 0		
14 3 9	30 5 0	45 15 0	33 10 0	38 0 0		
13 1 1	8 10 0	9 13 5	10 0 0	8 14 6		
117 0 5	161 15 0	278 4 11	792 10 0	823 4 0		

LONGFORD.

					Provisionally rented with other lands.	
80 0 32	74 0 0	110 0 0	96 0 0	73 0 0		
98 1 90	20 0 0	—	63 15 0	31 0 0	Provisionally rented with other lands.	
63 1 33	50 0 0	40 0 0	65 0 0	50 0 0		
39 1 9	25 5 0	33 19 0	97 0 0	31 12 4		
54 5 9	37 15 0	66 13 0	60 0 0	37 0 0		
17 3 10	14 5 0	20 0 0	17 0 0	13 0 0		
39 1 60	15 0 0	20 0 0	37 0 0	16 10 0		
1 3 43	1 5 0	4 0 0	3 5 0	1 4 0		
6 0 53	3 10 0	8 0 0	6 10 0	3 15 4		
11 0 23	1 10 0	11 0 0	6 0 0	5 1 0		
13 3 43	3 0 0	13 0 0	5 15 0	5 4 0		
6 3 97	1 5 0	8 0 0	4 10 0	3 10 0		
30 2 9	31 0 0	97 5 0	85 0 0	18 0 0		
65 0 20	37 15 0	63 0 0	61 0 0	40 10 0		
41 1 10	39 0 0	33 4 8	64 0 0	35 0 0		
50 2 15	64 0 0	97 10 0	39 8 5	33 10 0		
51 4 39	33 15 0	63 0 0	54 0 0	37 0 0		
45 1 5	40 10 0	60 0 0	63 0 0	45 0 0		
37 0 0	15 15 0	16 0 0	13 0 0	10 0 0		
67 1 93	23 5 0	39 11 8	56 0 0	51 0 0	Turbary at 2s. 6d. per Irish perch.
68 2 0	17 10 0	97 0 0	56 8 0	19 15 0	
60 2 0	50 15 0	47 3 6	*59 13 5	57 0 0	*Reduced to £56 14s. owing to a labourer's cottage plot being taken. Turbary at 2s. 6d. per Irish perch.
39 6 10	7 15 0	13 6 0	10 0 0	7 15 0	
40 3 13	71 5 0	86 16 4	23 0 0	19 10 0		
34 1 14	11 10 0	53 0 0	34 3 0	11 0 0		
901 5 86	561 15 0	542 5 2	695 0 0	560 17 0		

MAR

IRISH LAND COMMISSION.

SECOND STATUTORY TERM.

QUEEN'S

Name of Assistant Commissioners by whom Cases were decided.	Record Number.	Date of Order.	Name of Tenant.	Name of Landlord.	Townland.
Assistant Commissioners—		1897.			
R. T. CHEAT (Legal). F. M. GASKELL. J. HAVERTY.	13	March 17,	John Beggy,	Hon. Skeffington Town Shelton and others.	Grougerantulin
	13	„	William Whelan,	Mrs. Nannie Edge,	Ballyroddy,
	14	„	James Clancey,	do.	Gurtlagragh
	43	„	Daniel Ono,	Viscount De Vesci,	Rathnepin
	31	„	Richard Dunne,	Gerald FitzGerald,	Graiguenahown,
	80	„	Mary Byrne,	do.	do.
	23	„	James Walsh,	do.	do.
	31	„	Michael Maher,	Mrs. Jane F. Smyth-King,	Tourthea,
	63	„	Richard Butler,	Earl of Portarlington,	Sampson's Court
	64	„	Michael Mansfield,	do.	Moonfin,
	43	„	Peter R. Carter,	Robert H. Staples,	Cabar Castalin,
	34	„	Patrick Oxe,	do.	Wilderlig,
	23	„	Mary Fitzpatrick,	do.	do.
	31	„	Patrick Keye,	do.	Kilbeenly,
	43	„	Patrick Mansfield,	Gerald FitzGerald,	Graiguenahown,
	23	„	James Dwyer,	Viscount Ashbrook,	Knockahaun,
	37	„	William Keye,	do.	do.
	38	„	John Keye,	do.	do.
	33	„	Margaret Dunne,	do.	do.
	24	„	Patrick Cullen,	do.	do.
	63	„	John Heavey,	Robert H. Staples,	Cabar
	43	„	Andrew M'Evoy,	Mrs. Emily B. Hoyne,	Baloybeg
	40	„	James Delaney,	do.	do.
	33	„	Do.	do.	do.
	33	„	John Delaney,	do.	do.
	77	„	Daniel Delaney,	do.	do.
	13	„	James Clancey,	Mrs. Nannie Edge,	Ballyroddy,
	14	„	Do.	do.	Gurtlagragh
	51	„	John W. Wilkinson,	do.	Moyodd,
	8	„	Catherine Byrne,	do.	do.
					Total,

SECOND STATUTORY TERM.

COUNTY.

Amount of Building Ground	Poor Law Valuation	Deal of Holding paid in Creation of Fixed Statutory Term	Judicial Rent for First Statutory Term	Judicial Rent for Second Statutory Term	Observations	Value of Tenancy
£ s. d.	£ s. d.	£ s. d.	£ s. d.	£ s. d.		
22 3 11	14 15 0	23 1 5	16 16 0	16 10 0		
94 4 11	17 0 0	41 5 0	29 0 0	24 0 0		
7 3 73	2 15 0	13 17 6	8 10 0	5 5 0		
75 3 19	44 0 0	61 3 6	55 0 0	51 0 0		
9 3 55	5 10 0	8 15 0	6 0 0	6 14 6		
44 1 56	22 5 0	50 0 0	40 0 0	39 0 0		
33 3 3	34 5 0	30 15 4	28 0 0	27 13 6		
30 1 6	13 0 0	15 0 0	11 0 0	9 0 0		
16 0 17	11 5 0	13 0 0	10 15 0	9 15 0		
55 1 99	45 0 0	65 10 0	51 0 0	45 0 0		
41 1 7	37 15 0	38 0 0	55 0 0	40 10 0		
71 3 11	45 0 0	53 10 0	40 0 0	35 10 0		
101 0 29	91 5 0	144 5 0	115 0 0	97 15 0		
74 3 1	59 15 0	73 0 5	55 0 0	51 5 0		
5 1 0	4 0 0	—	7 13 5	4 0 0		
250 1 99	97 5 0	115 0 0	70 0 0	67 10 0		
45 0 20	17 0 0	37 5 0	23 0 0	17 5 0		
38 1 7	15 10 0	39 1 5	53 0 0	19 0 0		
19 1 35	9 10 0	15 15 5	11 0 0	9 5 0		
16 0 55	7 0 0	14 5 0	8 15 0	7 4 0		
45 3 9	23 15 0	30 0 0	51 15 5	25 11 0		
30 3 17	41 0 0	65 13 10	44 0 0	35 5 0		
55 1 5	35 10 0	61 5 0	50 0 0	35 0 0		
55 3 5	55 15 0	65 5 0	27 0 0	27 0 0		
55 0 0	55 5 0	55 0 0	45 0 0	32 11 5		
77 3 0	10 0 0	15 0 5	11 0 0	6 0 0		
1 3 10	1 15 0	2 5 0	1 17 6	1 17 6		
15 0 55	6 15 0	30 0 0	30 0 0	13 0 0		
155 1 54	55 0 0	305 15 0	230 0 0	165 0 0		
47 3 5	17 0 0	55 0 0	37 0 0	33 7 6		
1,575 0 50	657 10 0	1,546 11 11	1,139 0 0	917 15 0		

PROVINCE OF

SECOND STATUTORY TERM.

COUNTY OF

Name of Assistant Commissioners by whom Case was decided.	Record Number	Date of Order.	Name of Tenant.	Name of Landlord.	Townland.
AGRICULTURAL COMMISSIONERS—		1397.			
L. TOTTIE (Legal). C. O'KEEFFE. J. RICE.	69	March 12,	Patrick Conroy, junr.,	Mrs. Mary Ogilne,	Kilkenny,
	81	„	Patrick Conroy (Michl.)	do.	do.
	75	„	Michael Guthrie,	Thomas Crowe,	Fofrim,
	102	„	Nicholas Quinn,	Hyacinthe D'Arcy,	Ballinlahan,
	101	„	Patrick Donohoe,	do.	do.
	96	„	Peter Gibb,	do.	do.
	94	„	Mary McMahon,	do.	do.
	94	„	Catherine McMahon,	do.	Foxhun,
	93	„	Patrick Conroy, junr.,	do.	Kilkenny,
	97	„	Thomas Halloran,	Robert H. Crowe,	Lisnakinga,
	48	„	Daniel Gatroley,	Robert W. Ellis,	Kinahally,
	96	„	Andrew Hillery,	Alexander N. McEntire and others, Assignees of Chas. Vyse, deceased.	Carrowduff,
	89	„	Patrick Nagle,	do.	Carknduff,
	99	„	James O'Loughlin,	do.	Carrowduff,
	87	„	Do.	do.	Cahernderry,
	81	„	Patrick Foster,	do.	do.
	17	„	James Neylon, junior,	do.	do.
	19	„	Timothy Rormoyle,	do.	do.
	11	„	Michael Donlevy,	Mary Kenny and another,	Ballyea East,
	10	„	Michael Devine,	do.	do.
	18	„	James Neylon,	Alexander N. McEntire and others, Assignees of Chas. Vyse, deceased.	Cahernderry,
	13	„	Patrick Long,	Mary Kenny and mother, Reps. of Matthew Kenny,	Ballyea East,
	15	„	Thomas Ryan,	do.	Ballyea South,
	16	„	Mary Keatinge,	do.	do.
	17	„	Michael Lowery,	do.	do.
	103	„	Patrick Purtill,	Hyacinthe D'Arcy,	Ballinlahan,
	109	„	Thomas Quinn,	do.	do.

MUNSTER.

SECOND STATUTORY TERM.

CLARE.

Extent of Holding.	Poor Law Valuation.	Rent of Holding prior to sentice of Prov. Sentatory Term.	Judicial Rent for First Statutory Term.	Judicial Rent for Second Statutory Term.	Observations.	Value of Tenancy.
A. R. P.	£ s. d.	£ s. d.	£ s. d.	£ s. d.		£ s. d.

IRISH LAND COMMISSION
SECOND STATUTORY TERM.

COUNTY OF

Names of Assistant Commissioners by whom Case was decided	Record Number	Date of Cases	Name of Tenant	Name of Landlord	Townland
Assistant Commissioners—		1897.			
L. Doyle (Legal). C. O'Kelly. J. Bann.	99	March 12,	Bartholw. M'Mahon,	Mary Keary and another, Reps. of Matthew Keary,	Kyleaura,
	109	"	Patrick Rogery, ...	Madam Alude De La Hays,	Kilnamon, —
	75	"	John M. Shimken, ...	Stephen B. Wrath, ...	Thrranley, ...
	98	"	Owen Hagerty, ...	Mrs. Diana Stoddart, ...	Knockanelo, —
	67	"	Lott Halloran, ...	do.	do. —
	66	"	John Collins, ...	do.	Knockanelo, —
	64	"	Solomon Frost, ...	do.	Clappa Comb, —
	65	"	Michael M. O'Dea and another.	Lord Inchiquin, ...	Ballygannon, &c.
					Total, —

COUNTY OF

Assistant Commissioners—	154	March 23,	Patrick Fitzgerald, ...	Mary R. Hutton, ...	Oakarpul,
L. Doyle (Legal). R. G. Pool. E. Massey.					
L. Doyle (Legal). R. G. Pool.	179	"	Thomas Buckley, ...	Right Hon. Baron Cloriney,	Lackaragon,
	172	"	Daniel O'Sullivan, ...	do.	do.
	170	"	Matchins Kelly, ...	Richard Wall, ...	Oarnaheln,
	169	"	Denis Sullivan, ...	Henry L. Parley, ...	Farranstlg,
	166	"	Cortiss Harrigan, ...	Lord De Vesci, ...	Monkstown and another,
	168	"	Do.	do. ...	Monkstown.
					Total,

COUNTY OF

Assistant Commissioners—	69	March 17,	James Houlihan. ...	Lord Ventry, ...	... Kerry, ...
L. Doyle (Legal). A. N. Crew. J. A. Bampton.	85	"	John McCabe, junior,	Earl of Kenmare,	Knockbrack,
	96	"	Ellen McCabe, Admix. of Michael McCabe,	do.	Castletown,
					Total,

SECOND STATUTORY TERM.

CLARE—continued.

Amount of Holding, Ireland.	Poor Law Valuation.	Rent of Holding prior to creation of First Statutory Term.	Judicial Rent for First Statutory Term.	Judicial Rent for Second Statutory Term.	Observations.	Value of Tenancy.
A. R. P.	£ s. d.	£ s. d.	£ s. d.	£ s. d.		£ s. d.
73 3 0	16 10 0	19 16 3	19 10 0	18 0 0		
63 1 52	31 6 0	35 0 0	34 0 0	30 0 0		
90 0 10	31 10 0	30 0 0	13 0 0	10 7 0		
19 1 80	8 5 0	17 10 0	11 0 0	9 9 0		
82 1 39	11 0 0	18 0 0	11 10 0	7 5 0		
30 8 89	8 12 0	13 0 0	9 10 0	7 0 0		
93 1 5	53 0 0	180 0 0	93 0 0	67 8 0		
398 0 4	66 0 0	110 0 0	66 0 0	88 0 0		
7,491 1 6	653 17 0	950 9 3	716 0 0	530 8 0		

CORK.

37 8 19	67 10 0	110 0 0	110 0 0	83 13 6		
94 1 37	81 0 0	57 0 0	44 0 0	37 0 0		
45 0 15	13 15 0	13 0 0	34 0 0	75 17 6		
43 0 0	77 5 0	65 0 0	58 8 0	26 7 6		
133 1 . 0	19 0 0	121 4 6	109 0 0	73 8 0		
33 3 31	60 0 0	46 0 0	44 0 0	39 8 0		
11 1 98	14 15 0	80 0 0	50 0 0	16 13 6		
661 3 31	803 5 0	646 8 3	534 0 0	301 0 0		

KERRY.

64 1 13	35 0 0	65 0 0	45 0 0	30 10 0	With an undivided 3rd of 17l. 3s. 57r.	
137 1 41	48 9 0	44 0 0	64 0 0	45 10 0		
100 3 0	51 15 0	110 0 0	100 0 0	84 10 0		
301 3 34	135 4 0	945 0 0	279 0 0	144 10 8		

CIVIL BILL

PROVINCE OF

SECOND STATUTORY TERM.

COUNTY OF

County Court Judge.	Record Number.	Date of Order.	Name of Tenant.	Name of Landlord.	Townland.
O. WALTER, Q.C.		1891.			
	62	Jan. 30,	Kate Boylan,	R. E. Freehill	Garrycam,
	71	Jan. 31,	William Donohoe,	Mary R. Buchanan,	Darragh & one,
	72	„	Patrick Donohoe,	do.	Darragh,
	60	„	John M'Adam,	Hon. Chas. Annesley,	Anghurahelle,
	75	„	Catherine Prior,	Richard Kelly,	Mullaghdun,
	66	„	Mary Maguire,	Arthur J. Crawford,	Aughnahinagh,
	67	„	Charles Maguire,	do.	do.
	68	„	Thomas Kiernan,	John Black,	Rantavanagh,
	17	„	Catherine Prior,	Earl Annesley,	Sheepbring's,
					Total

PROVINCE OF

COUNTY OF

W. H. NERNY, Q.C.	5	Feb. 6,	Owen Murphy,	Hon. Katherine Plunkett and others,	Lowrath,
	4	„	John Kellely,	do.	Carrickmakan
					Total

PROVINCE OF

COUNTY OF

O. WALTER, Q.C.	29	Jan. 15,	James Regan,	Mary Parks and others,	Aughrunkan
	76	„	Do.	do.	do.
	61	Jan. 7,	Patrick Kenny,	Lord Massy,	Oakmanvalan,
	40	„	Patrick Kenny (John),	do.	do.

COURTS.

ULSTER.

CAVAN.

Extent of Holding	Poor Law Valuation	Rent of Holding prior to making of First Statutory Term	Judicial Rent for First Statutory Term	Judicial Rent for Second Statutory Term	Observations	Value of Tenancy
a. r. p.	£ s. d.	£ s. d.	£ s. d.	£ s. d.		£ s. d.
33 0 9	19 0 0	37 10 0	23 0 0	18 10 0		
67 1 5	47 0 0	69 11 0	53 0 0	40 0 0		
39 6 27	11 0 6	16 18 0	13 0 0	9 10 0		
16 3 6	15 6 0	17 6 0	12 6 0	6 0 0		
8 2 39	6 0 0	8 6 0	9 0 0	3 16 0		
56 8 96	7 10 0	16 10 0	16 10 0	8 0 0		
39 9 16	1 6 0	6 0 0	6 0 6	4 10 0		
16 0 0	9 15 0	—	11 10 0	4 16 0		
9 3 23	9 10 0	11 5 4	9 19 6	6 10 0		
776 3 28	126 3 0	177 6 4	138 6 6	105 10 0		

LEINSTER.

LOUTH.

4 1 0	8 0 0	13 6 5	10 0 0	6 6 6		
17 3 16	12 15 0	14 0 0	15 10 0	10 3 6		
21 1 16	20 15 0	29 5 5	25 10 0	16 6 0		

CONNAUGHT.

LEITRIM.

16 2 33	7 16 0	14 15 6	9 10 0	6 6 0		
13 3 26	6 15 0	13 5 6	7 10 0	4 16 0		
107 0 13	50 0 0	23 0 0	19 10 0	12 0 0		
25 1 17	7 0 0	6 9 0	6 2 0	5 12 0		

SECOND STATUTORY TERM.

COUNTY OF

County Court Judge.	Record Number.	Date of Order.	Name of Tenant.	Name of Landlord.	Townland.
G. Waters, q.c.	41	1897. Jan. 7,	Mary Ferry, Rep. of Bridget M'Auley.	Sarah Ashmore and another,	Tattinanny, ...
	10	"	Dan M'Auley, ...	do.	do. ...
	39	"	Hugh Flynn, ...	do.	do. ...
	8	"	Fartley Gordon, ...	C. C. Tottenham & another, Trustees of Sarah Ann Tottenham.	Legnanouny,
	56	"	John M'Morrow, ,,	do.	Stranagran, ...
	57	"	Peter M'Garry, ...	do.	do. ...
	86	"	John Kelly, ...	do.	do. ...
	74	"	Christopher Smart, ...	do.	Glankeel, ...
	72	"	Cormack Gaffney, ...	do.	Ballyboy, ...
	2	"	John Maeas, ...	do.	Killyvingan, ...
	2	"	Pat M'Hugh, Rep. of Pat M'Hugh, decd.	do.	Langfarm, ...
	1	"	Thomas M'Hugh, Rep. of Pat M'Hugh, decd.	do.	do. ...
	8	"	Felix M'Hugh, Rep. of Pat M'Hugh, decd.	do.	Langfarm & anr., ...
					Total. ...

PROVINCE OF

COUNTY OF

County Court Judge.					
W. S. Brann, q.c.	71	Jan. 14,	Denis Leary,	Munster and Leinster Bank, Limited.	Ballyackwes, ...
	87	Jan. 22,	John Foley, ...	Moreton Powers, ...	Inchykingley, ...
	33	"	George Stanley, ...	do.	do. ...
	88	Jan. 14,	Timothy Murphy, ...	James Michem.	Caprahere, ...
	84	Jan. 22,	T. J. Bramich,	Col. Biggs Baldwin,	Clotanemmore, ...
	36	"	Do. ...	do. ".	do. ...
	93	Jan. 14,	D. J. Leary, ...	Mrs. Margaret Banker,	Glanvan West, ...
J. G. Naughar, q.c.	96	Jan. 16,	Denis Lahune,	John W. B. Creagh,	Clearihan, ...
	37	"	John Harding, ...	do. ...	do. ...
	94	"	John Riordan, ...	do. ...	do. ...

SECOND STATUTORY TERM.

LEITRIM—continued.

Extent of Holding, Statute	Poor Law Valuation.	Rent of Holding prior to cessation of Poor Law Statutory Term.	Judicial Rent for First Statutory Term.	Judicial Rent for Second Statutory Term.	Observations.	Value of Tenancy.
	£ s. d.	£ s. d.	£ s. d.	£ s. d.		£ s. d.

MUNSTER.

CORK.